CHALLENGING BURKE
Embrace Island

ACI Unleashed Book 2

★ ★ ★

Olivia Sinclair

Get a free book!

Join my newsletter and get another ACI-related story available only to subscribers.

https://BookHip.com/ZNBSVAS

1

Cassidy

I know I've got a seriously geeky side although I never thought I'd cream my panties over a piece of tech. But that little drone is fine. As soon as they call for volunteers, I'm not only raising my hand, but I stand up and walk to the podium. Up close it's even more impressive. It's a true micro drone, not compromising on any of the bells and whistles. It's got a full HDR video stream, audio, night vision and it fits in the palm of my hand. Who wouldn't want to play with that?

There are some grins and giggles behind me, but not from the woman with the microphone who is wearing a peach suit that is vastly inappropriate for the muddy environment, matching heels, and a concerned expression. "Are you sure, um," she glances down at my nametag, "Cassidy? This might be a great opportunity for you to break through some barriers?" She really says that last bit as if she knows me personally and thinks I'm shy.

I'm perplexed for a minute, wondering if she's confused me with someone else before it hits me. Oh, my face. I'm so over other people somehow thinking it's all new to me. "No, I want that drone." I look her straight in the eye and dare her to challenge me on it further. Her gaze drops, and she steps back.

And I do want it. I have serious plans for that little baby, not all of them on the up and up. But HR lady who's determined to make me feel like a victim of society or genetics or something doesn't need to know that.

A few other women who weren't quite so bold come up when they're called (after raising their hands) and join me. They look nervous and excited — I think this might be pushing at their comfort boundaries already, but I can't wait to get started. My older brothers are going to be so jealous when I tell them. Hopefully, all the details aren't classified because that would be a real bummer. It's rare that I have better stories to tell than they do. I don't want to miss my chance at the next family get together.

Another woman comes up and hands each of us a few sheets of paper with basic instructions on where to go and what our mission will be. Then she takes our names and tent assignments. All told it's a group of five that become the mini drone squad. We start training in the morning.

Once that's squared away, I return to my uncomfortable gray metal folding chair at the back of the tent and let the rest of the presentation roll over me. My role for the next two weeks has been determined so I don't feel a great need to pay attention to how to seduce a man the HR-approved way. Which quite frankly sounds ridiculous and like something out of a 1950s video about being an 'asset' as a decorative secretary. No touching, no nudity, but batting eyelashes is fine. Blah, blah, blah.

The woman next to me mutters "fucking idiots" under her breath. I turn to her with a grin that she returns with an embarrassed whisper, "Sorry!"

I turn back so I'm facing forward but whisper to her out of the corner of my mouth, "Do you think anyone follows these stupid rules?"

She snorts softly. "Maybe that woman up there in the front row, the one with the ruffles."

My eyes trail along the row of chairs far in front of us to see who she's talking about. Oh. Her. There's a woman of indeterminate age, at least from the back, whose street clothes consist of what looks like a pink and green ruffled pinafore. Her dark hair is in some kind of fancy braided up do. "Probably a stripper," I whisper back to my neighbor, who giggles loudly before slapping a hand over her mouth.

"I'm Violet, by the way," she says softly when she regains control.

"Cassidy," I respond back.

"Want to get lunch together? I'm not sure I can take much more political correctness."

"Sure. Is it coming soon?"

I can hear the smile in her voice. "The schedule says fifteen minutes."

Well, they have been keeping to a schedule like it really is the military. Which it isn't, but try telling that to any of the testosterone jocks employed by ACI.

The lady doing the talking starts going faster as if she can see a countdown clock and has to get through all her words before then. Her razor-cut blonde bob swings with her fierce enthusiasm over personal growth. And maybe there is a clock because there's a soft gong and suddenly everyone is on their feet, heading to the aisles as if they were poised on the edge of their seats, just waiting for the signal. I exchange a look with Violet who now that we're standing is about a half a foot shorter than me and cute as a button. I'll bet she hates that. Her dark hair is making perfect corkscrew curls. I have no idea if it's always that way or just doing something special because of the humidity. Already I've noticed my own hair has taken on a life of its own. I've yet to decide if that's a good thing.

It's just starting to rain outside, big swaths of mist moving between the large evergreens on the edge of the compound. I can't wait to explore the woods here because I hear there are no poisonous critters to watch out for, but I have yet to set foot in them. I guess you can't have trees growing up right against the runway.

We follow the crowd to the big mess hall, which is in another giant tent two down from where we were being held in HR purgatory. And wouldn't you know it, all those military guys got there first. They already have filled most of the cafeteria tables, and the last few men are making their way through the lines.

"Fuckers," I mutter. I'll bet they knew when we would be arriving and timed the end of their presentations to finish five minutes earlier. We'll be lucky if there's any food left.

There is, but it's mostly 'girl food' as in salads and fruit smoothies. Violet and I exchange eye rolls before filling our trays with what we can find and claiming one of the tables that's already being vacated by big, tough men dressed in green camo. I eye their retreating backs, wondering if any of them are about to report to me.

That's part of my personal secret mission. I've been given a promotion. Only just last week and it's not been made public yet. And I'm scared out of my ever-loving mind because not only am I five years younger than the youngest person on my new team but they're all combat veterans. I don't talk that talk and I definitely don't walk the walk. But now I'm their boss, well I will be in three weeks' time. And three of the five men are here at the war games somewhere.

I know their names and I've read their files, but I don't know their assignments here. I'm hoping I can figure that out tonight when they post all the 'meet your teammates' stuff that they've promised. Then I'm going to do a little spying that has nothing to do with the games' objective of capturing Airstrip #1. All the big tents are pitched on the tarmac of Airstrip #2 so at least that won't be a point of confusion. I hope. Some of these guys look tough but like maybe they don't have that much processing capacity. I'm desperate to get a sense of the men reporting to me before they know I'm watching, so I have some idea of what I'm up against. I know I can't be their buddy, but I'd like it if it didn't have to be all out war. And it shouldn't be. I mean, I want them to succeed and I want to succeed too. Shouldn't be in conflict, right?

Burke

Getting old sucks. It's not the number, or even the subtle creaking in my knees, it's my damn response time going down by whole seconds. Even when I work out an extra hour a day and feel fitter than I ever have. The clock doesn't lie. And the time on the clock says I'm no longer the fastest rescue swimmer in or out of the Navy. Not by a lot. And I'm starting to feel the cold in ways I didn't ten years ago.

I know what that means, my support staff know

what that means. Retirement to another job or the dreaded coaching position held by so many former champions. I haven't decided which one I hate least but I've got about two weeks to make up my mind. Because while I might be able to continue rescue swimming in low-risk environments like this one, where it's unlikely anything serious is going to happen, the days of high seas adventures are clearly over. Part of me says fine, let the next generation suck in too much salt water and bang sharks on the nose. And another side of me rails against fate, mostly because nothing more exciting has come along to lure me into my forties with enthusiasm.

I'm bored.

It doesn't help that I've got this little two-person tent by the water's edge to myself. Pablo, the other swimmer who's supposed to relieve me on duty, having decided that this tent is much too far away from the female contingent, has removed himself to the big barracks. He won't get any sleep but can leer at girls over breakfast first thing. Or something. If he thinks he's getting any, he hasn't figured out that the women are also in group tents and don't have any privacy. Or maybe that doesn't bother him. I don't care enough to find out.

I'm stretched out on my narrow cot, staring up at the khaki fabric ceiling, wondering how long before the rain pounding on it starts to seep through. No sign of it yet, but I don't see canvas winning the battle against Mother Nature. At this point, this is the most exciting thing I have to look forward to.

A high-pitched buzzing catches my attention and my first thought is a mosquito, because what else could add more pain and irritation to the day now that it's almost over? But when I glance around, trying to track the microscopic motherfucker, I see a drone instead.

It's tiny. I didn't even know drones came that small — about the size of a small apple, complete with a blinking red eye and four little rotors. I watch it move across the tent towards the stack of reading material I was given. Not all my reflexes are gone to shit because I'm able to upend a water glass over it with minimal effort. The glass was empty, so I doubt any damage was done to the drone. Now I can take my time figuring out who the fuck is spying on me and why.

I mean I know this is a war games but I'm here purely in a support capacity in case of emergency, not part of the assigned feuding sides. Which means I should be about as boring as it can get to anyone looking for intel. Maybe the little drone is just lost. Except as Pablo pointed out multiple times, this tent really is a long way away from everything else. Huh.

The tiny machine is hopping and buzzing, trying to shift the glass off the stack of books through sheer force of will. It makes me smile watching it. The glass is heavy, and the drone isn't. Eventually it settles down as if waiting for something, and I eye it cautiously. I want to examine it more closely, but not at the expense of having it fly away. I'll check it in the morning. Surely those things have batteries that will wear down by then?

I'm feeling more energetic now just having something new to think about, so I decide to change into running clothes and head out for a jog on the beach. I'm used to running in the rain. If anything, it's invigorating, and it tends to keep everyone else out of my way. I'm committed to this plan until I strip down. With my pants down around my knees I'm startled by the furious buzzing of the tiny drone. It whirrs back to life and turns around, its red light blinking furiously at the wall.

For the first time in forever, I laugh so hard I have to sit down. Who knew drones could be embarrassed by human nudity? And honestly, I've spent so much of my life parading around in nothing more than a tiny lycra bathing suit that I don't think too much of it with humans either. I mean, I usually remember to put on more clothes to go to the grocery store, but not always. They fucking mean that no shirt, no service thing, so I've had to resort to keeping spares in my car because I'm always forgetting when I live in a warmer climate.

So this little dot of tech practically blushing is fucking hilarious. And it means only one thing. There's a girl on the other end of it, I'd bet my life on it. And now my interest in jogging has flown out the window and I want to know more about her and why she's flown a micro drone into my tent. I mean, I really want to know. I snag a pair of sleep pants that I brought thinking it might be cold here and pull them on. I've no idea if the drone has audio but I'll bet it does so I say as gently as I can, "You can turn around now. I'm decent."

There's a long pause and then it slowly and almost reluctantly rotates back 180 degrees. The rotors are still spinning, but I ignore that and sit back down on my cot. Time to do a little research into all the propaganda they send out for these things.

It takes ten minutes but I finally find it. And I'm quirking an eyebrow at the drone while staring at it. It's not moving, but I feel like it's watching me. I glance down at the paperwork again. According to this, any drone operator who loses physical control of his or her drone for twenty-four consecutive hours is declared 'dead'. The same as if they were shot by one of the paintball guns. My drone girl is in some serious shit. And I'll bet my cozy little tent that she'll be by sometime later tonight to try to reclaim her equipment. Which means if I want to get a good look at her and find out her name, I've got some work to do.

"Sorry, sweetheart," I say cheerfully as I drop a towel over the glass-covered drone and then I move it and the stack of books over into the far corner.

Next I reposition the cots so that the only way to the drone is over my bed. And I double check the back walls to make sure there's no easy point of entry under them either. Just to be safe, I put a box over the drone ensemble and pile some more shit on top.

Now for the girl. I've no idea what size she might be, but it's highly unlikely I can't take her. But I don't have anything to restrain her with, like handcuffs, and I doubt very much she'll be in the mood to sit and chat. I eye my jacket and assorted other crap lying around. I'm not exactly neat — and don't believe what those recruitment posters tell anxious mothers. Yeah, I used to get in trouble on a regular basis for my mess, but that never made me any neater. I suppose I could smother her in clothes, tie the arms together or something. I don't want to hurt her, so sitting on her seems like not a great idea.

It would really help if I had some idea of who she is. I flip back through all the materials and even look online. But there are too many people and no mention of drones. Must have been something that was doled out on site. Guess I'll just have to be patient for a few more hours.

Cassidy

How could I be so stupid? Not only have I lost control of my drone — on the first day — but the guy who has it is unbelievably panty-melting hot. Like seriously the most beautiful man I've ever seen in my life that wasn't on a TV screen. And I'm not entirely sure I haven't seen him on one. I actually caught myself drooling when I saw the definition of his abs and that err, what was below that. I only just managed to turn the drone around in time. Yes, I could have turned it off or looked away, but I couldn't make my fingers or eyes do those actions. And to be honest, I wasn't done looking at him. I just didn't need to see him quite that naked. But his shoulders? I could look at those for days. Broad and smoothly muscled — just yum.

But the worst part is how am I supposed to be a manager to that? He doesn't look anything like the small photo in his employee file. And believe me, I know how sexist that sounds. But if I were a man having this problem with a woman, people would just smirk and pat me on the back. A woman who secretly lusts after her subordinate is just sneered at. And my guess is, he'll figure it out and take full advantage of it by never listening to me unless it suits his interests. I am so screwed.

I'm hyperventilating while sitting here on my assigned cot, all while getting strange looks from the other women rushing around, getting ready for bed, and setting things out for tomorrow. I haven't met any of them. Violet is staying in another tent and the other women working drones are billeted elsewhere too. Just as well because I don't really want it getting out that I don't have control of my drone at the moment.

"You alright, there? Cassidy, wasn't it?" A lanky woman with a strong jaw and amber eyes stops in front of me, a concerned expression softening the stern angles of her face.

"Yeah, just learned something unpleasant. I'll be fine once I process." I make an effort to smile back so she won't linger, but she does anyway.

"Anybody giving you shit?"

"Not in here."

She nods cautiously like she wants to say something further, but isn't ready to cross that line just yet. "I'm Lenny. If you need me, I'm bunked in that far corner." She points and I incline my head with a smile as she turns away.

I appreciate that she didn't try to make a big deal of trying to be instant best friends. I've had more than enough self-indulgent offers of camaraderie in my life to usually spot them at the first word. Lenny was being sincere and not pushing. If I wasn't so busy kicking myself, I'd make more of an effort to being friendly in return.

I have to pull myself together. In another hour it will be dark enough to go and retrieve Betsy. Which is the name I've given my drone. It just seems friendlier than N-760-AL109. She has a tracking device that I can orient to from my phone so I don't have to search all over the compound, but the signal is weakened by whatever this guy Jason Burke put over it. My map is saying it's right on the edge of the signal so I need to work fast. Hopefully I'll be back here and sleeping peacefully in a little under two hours, three at the max. But it's been raining so boots and a flashlight are a necessity as well as some other gear. I breathe deep several times and force myself into the present and the problems I can deal with today. Like retrieving Betsy.

When the overhead lights go out promptly at 9 pm, I stand up and put on my rain gear. I have my cellphone and a small flashlight and that's it. Anything else might bog me down or worse, get me caught. I'm hoping Jason is asleep when I get there and I can get in and get out smoothly. If not, I might have to wait outside in the rain until he is. There are soft amber lights illuminating the 'baseboards' of the tent I'm in, so it's not hard to make it to the front door without disturbing anyone. I don't envy the women sleeping by the wooden door though. It's bound to be swinging too and fro throughout the night since the bathroom (or latrine in military lingo) is outside. And yes, they're portable toilets and yes, they already smell to high heaven.

I scoot past them as quickly as I can, taking the wider path that leads in the general direction of the inlet at the tip of the island. That's where my destination is, although why he's set up so far away from everything I'll probably never know. The guy is a project manager, why does he need to be near the beach and half a mile away from everyone else? Oh God, I hope he's not dangerous. But surely if he was, they wouldn't have assigned him here, or to report to me? Would they? Remembering HR lady with her penchant for stretching 'barriers' I'm not so sure.

A shiver runs down my spine. Maybe I'm about to be seriously stupid. It's not too late to turn back. I almost do when an owl hoots long and low, and for the life of me I can't tell what direction it came from. I always thought I was at home in nature but out here in the wet with no light because of the heavy cloud cover, I'm not so confident. But something in me refuses to give up, to take the safe way, and I turn my flashlight to high and keep walking.

The thighs of my jeans are soaked through and my boots are squishing in the mud, threatening to pull off my feet completely if I'm not careful. I slow down and then I see it finally, just a hint of an outline in the deep gloom. A tent. Not a typical camping tent, but an old school military one like you see in the movies with a wooden infrastructure. In a way that's good, because it will give me more maneuverability. I stop where I am and turn off my flashlight. Then I take out my phone and dim the screen as best I can. I need to check if my drone is still online and if this is in fact the right location. It is. The signal is a little stronger since I'm standing nearby, so I can tell it's in the tent, but not which corner or anything more specific. I move forward slowly. I really can't see where I'm going, but I don't want to alert the occupant to my presence.

In what seems like forever later, I'm finally standing outside the slatted wooden door. I ease it open just a fraction so I can peek inside. It's completely dark. I can't make out any blinking lights from a phone or a computer, nothing. I turn my ear to the crack and listen. Deep, even breathing. He's asleep. Good. I flick my flashlight to the lowest possible setting and scan the interior of the tent, doing my best not to cast the light over the large body in the cot right inside the door. Why on earth does he have his bed there? Wouldn't it be easier to come and go if it were up against one of the sides?

I scream when large hands pull me down onto the bed, my flashlight flying into the far corner with a thunk.

"Easy there, princess." A low growly voice grunts in my ear when I manage to connect my foot with some part of my attacker's anatomy. "Let's not rule out having kids just yet, okay?"

Burke

Well, I'm not bored anymore. It's entirely possible I may never be again.

I've yet to get a look at drone girl but I've had a very good feel thanks to her attempting to escape. And I've got nothing to complain about. I finally settle on bracing myself on my elbows, which gives her room to breathe but also keeps her from being able to maneuver to hit me very hard. She's still making a lot of effort to get a few whacks in, but they don't hurt. Much.

I take a minute to scoot her up in my bed because the way my cock is reacting to her, I don't need her thinking I'm going to attack her. He's just a little excited at the way she's moving around. With my waist settled between her thighs, she still tries to bang on my butt with her boots, so I reach one long arm back and tug them off.

"Now you can kick as much as you like, princess. But could you maybe share why you're in my tent while you do it? I'd like to get some sleep eventually."

"Let me go!"

"So you can grab your drone and disappear into the night like Cinderella? I don't think so. Half the women here could fit into those muddy boots you were wearing. Take too long to find you. Start talking."

She stills beneath me and I'm not clear if she's trying to take me by surprise or if she's thinking about what to say. Both apparently because she gives a sudden surprise shove with both palms flat on my chest that goes precisely nowhere. Then she starts rambling.

"Look, I can't explain. Really, it's better for both of us if I don't. My life will be much easier if you don't recognize me when you officially meet me. Seriously. Just let me go, Jason, please?"

Whoa. "Who the hell is Jason?" Unbelievably I'm suddenly jealous and determined to make sure this Jason character ceases to exist in her world. Besides, I'm starting to feel a little too comfortable and relaxed between her thighs. I might already be addicted.

"You are? Jason Burke. This is his tent."

"No, it isn't, princess. This is the tent of one Burke Jamieson. Well, and Pablo Duarte officially but he's made other arrangements."

"Not Jason Burke, a project manager in IT?" She sounds adorably hopeful.

"No. Burke Jamieson, current rescue swimmer about to be God knows what, at your service."

"Oh, thank fuck." Her deep sigh of relief seems to take all the fight right out of her.

"Sooo, princess. Do I get a name and maybe an explanation?"

"Um, you can't just let me go with my drone? It was an innocent mistake."

"So you can go look at fucking Jason Burke naked? I don't think so, princess."

"I really, really don't want to see him naked. Or you either." She assures me hurriedly, but I can feel the heat of her pussy against my middle, and I know she's lying about the last part. At least I think she is.

"Talk."

"Um, well, see, I'm about to become a manager. And the guys reporting to me, well they're all older and from what I can tell tough guys."

I'm liking this less and less, but I hold my growls of protest in for the moment.

"So I wanted to get a little advance intel on them, figure out what I'd be dealing with in a few weeks. See how they behave in their natural environment."

I grunt. I can understand her motivation if not her execution. But I don't have to like any of it.

"I don't understand how I confused Jason Burke with you though." She sounds bewildered.

"Princess, what's your name?"

She's silent for a long time before she finally relents with another small sigh, "Cassidy."

Guess I'm not getting a last name out of her tonight. I can work with Cassidy, it's not common enough to be too confusing. There can't be more than a handful of them working at ACI.

"Baby, a drone is one thing, but did you seriously consider how dangerous it is to enter a strange man's tent late at night?"

"You mean he might accost me and hold me prisoner?" Her tone has gone sarcastic, and I love it.

I grin down at her in the darkness. "Exactly. Only I'm the nice kind of jailer. And there's no way in hell I would ever take orders from you, princess."

She stiffens again. "What the hell does that mean? Do you have some kind of problem with women in authority?"

I think about it for a minute. "No, don't think so. I

had a female CO for a while. She was fine. Barked the same orders as the men did." I shrug, missing those days of being stationed in high alert situations, just waiting for the mission specifics before hitting the water hard.

"Then what's so special about me?"

"Well, for starters, I don't see myself ever taking work orders from my wife. The ones for harder, longer, faster, sure." I grin again at her splutter of outrage. "Or even turning the Christmas tree for the five hundredth time until it's perfect, but telling me to redo my expense report because I left off a receipt? Not so much. And besides, pretty sure there are rules about being married to your boss these days."

"Where in your little fantasy world did we get married? You haven't even ever seen me."

"Well, that's true. But even if you're hideous looking, which I doubt, you're the most entertaining woman to ever be in my bed. So thinking I want to keep you here. And your body is telling me you're not completely averse to the idea. I get that you might want to see me with more clothes on at some point but I'm just letting you know my intentions."

She's quiet and I'm about ready to reach for the light when she says softly, "A lot of men do think I'm rather hideous looking. I happen to think they're idiots so there are no hard feelings but just so you know."

Damn, I am good at putting my foot in my mouth. I need her to explain what this means to her. "Cass?"

"I have a birthmark on the left side of my face, I don't even notice it anymore, I mean it's always been a part of me so it's like noticing I have brown eyes. But some people have been known to come up to me from the right with a smile, get the full picture, and keep walking with well, not a smile."

I'm torn here. I want to physically hurt anyone that's ever tried to make her feel bad about herself and on the other hand, I'm sorta grateful for anything that's kept her single until I could find her. "You are single, right?" I ask her out of the blue, realizing I might have overlooked one critical detail in my plans to keep her forever.

"That's what you got out of that soul-bearing confession? That I'm probably single?" She sounds both amused and outraged.

"No, I was feeling ready to rend all those men limb from limb, but decided I didn't want them around you anyway. That's when I realized I'd assumed that someone that was too embarrassed to see me naked even via a drone camera must be single. So are you?"

"Embarrassed or single?"

"Princess," I warn her with a fraction more of my weight on her.

"Oooph, you're heavy. I'm very single. My brothers would say it has way more to do with my bossy attitude than my face. Happy?"

"With that answer, yes. For now."

3

Cassidy

Okay, I'm willing to admit that I might have one or two unresolved trust issues. I happen to think a healthy amount of skepticism is a sign of intelligence. But just now I'm feeling this uncontrollable urge to rip the band-aid off because Burke is so charming in his bossy alpha attitude. And his weight over me is so primally delicious that I think I could get my heart hurt. Not broken, I've never been a believer in love at first sight, but lightly bruised is seeming more and more likely. So if he's not as awesome as he seems, I'd rather find out sooner than later.

Although when is that ever not true? Does anyone out there think, 'well gee, don't tell me my man is a lying, cheating scumbag until we've been together ten years?' I doubt it. Anyway, like a sore tooth I'm suddenly needing to get the whole face-to-face thing out of the way, but I have to make him turn on a light or let me get up. And for some reason it's easier to say it all in the dark, anyway.

"So, are you planning to stay on top of me all night? I've said I'm sorry."

"Uh, no. You didn't. And I was thinking morning would be soon enough to return you to wherever you came from, yes."

"Fine, I'm sorry I spied on you, and I'm sorry I entered your tent without knocking. Better?"

"Very nicely done. I accept your apology."

"Then why aren't you moving?"

"Because I'm not sorry you did any of those things?"

I snort, not following his logic at all.

"So tell me something, Cassidy."

"Something."

"Smartass. If there were a safe, no side effects medical procedure to erase your birthmark, would you do it?"

My stomach drops. His voice is quiet, not brash and demanding, which is at odds with how I first hear the question. I make myself pause and take a deep breath. "No, I wouldn't. It's part of me, part of my history. When I was much younger yes, I'd have done that in a heartbeat because fitting in seemed like the only path to success but not now." And I wait to see how he takes that because I'm really not sure.

"Yeah, like me and my teeth."

"Your teeth?"

"I'm not saying it's the same thing just that I have these two teeth that stick out a bit and for years people were trying to get me to fix 'em. Make me look perfect, or like everyone else, I was never quite sure. But they kept banging on about it and even said I'd make more money on endorsements. That's when I told them to fuck the endorsements and joined the Navy. Might have been a bit of an extreme response but I don't regret it."

"You went into the Navy because a few people insulted your teeth?"

"It was a bit more than that. I had been going to wait until after the Olympics but I finally got so fed up with it I said fuck it and made the move early."

"Wait, you were going to go to the Olympics, and you turned that down?"

"Yeah, well, I'd qualified, but they were still almost a year away and honestly, I didn't much see the point. Beyond the money and endorsements."

"But it's the Olympics." I'm so confused by this man.

"And I'm seriously value goal oriented, Cassidy. You should know that about me. Winning and going fast is fun but ultimately it doesn't really contribute anything meaningful, at least not to me. If it does for other people great, some other guy got a chance for that when I stepped aside. But you know what I did in that time between joining the Navy and when the Olympics happened?"

"Uh, whatever the equivalent is to army boot camp?"

"Yeah, that too. But I saved eight lives, Cass. Eight people that desperately needed help I could give. And the swimming was a lot more exciting than going in a straight line too."

"I was planning on being a superhero when I was eight," I confess, not really sure where this conversation is going or why I'm revealing this now. But it seems important to get it out.

"Yeah? Which one?"

"Africa Girl."

"Can't say as I've heard of her."

"You wouldn't have. She was my invention. Because my birthmark just happens to be the exact shape of the east coast of Africa. And I was pretty damn excited to discover that in Mrs. Grant's geography class."

"Huh, so what stopped you? Unless you currently are a superhero. But then I think you'd be better at sneaking into tents."

For that snarky remark, I give him a kick with my stocking foot, but he doesn't even react. "Well, Mrs.

Grant wasn't a fan. She said it was inappropriate and why didn't I be Friendship Girl instead."

"I'm guessing by your tone that was a no-go."

"Maybe if I'd had a flower on my face but when you're eight being different special is a lot more exciting than being different weird. Now I think they're pretty much the same thing."

"So you didn't just give up?"

"Hell no, I went home and drew up my costume."

"Which was?"

"Purple with a big pink A on the front."

"Makes sense, why am I sensing deep tragedy ahead for Africa Girl?"

"Because my mother said absolutely no to anything with an A on the front."

"Why? She have something against the first letter of the alphabet? When all the superheroes lined up for lunch, you would have been first."

"Right? Guess that means you haven't read the Scarlet Letter either. Apparently wearing an A means you're a slut, according to my mother anyway. And it doesn't even matter if it's not red. She put her foot down."

"Princess, I can't take it anymore. I need to see this for myself."

I can feel him moving a hand around and before long I see a tiny penlight barely bigger than a pencil. For some reason I'm expecting a full facial scan, but he keeps the light just to the hairline on the left side of my face. I can't even see his expression as he studies the coloration of my skin.

"I totally see it. But… you're missing Madagascar."

"I know. I tried to fix that with the brown whiteboard marker. Mrs. Grant got very upset."

"I'm starting to not like Mrs. Grant. What was her problem this time? I'd have thought she'd have been pleased with your attention to geographic detail."

"You know, I never really found out. My mother just kept saying 'she means well' which is what she said about my great aunt Phyllis who was always dropping off her church magazines at our house."

Burke flips the light back off and I feel a light touch on my throat right about where Madagascar would be. "I could fix it for you, temporarily anyway."

I gulp because there's something decidedly suggestive in his voice, but I'm not following at all. "What do you mean?"

Instead of answering with words, he brings his head down and suddenly my skin is ablaze as his lips suck lightly on that spot, just under my jawline. A bolt of lightening shoots down my core, setting everything on fire.

"When you're ready, princess." He raises his head up again and suddenly I feel exposed, like I've been under a cozy blanket that someone suddenly rips away.

"Um," is all I can manage.

I can feel his whole body smile in response. "So, did you have any superpowers?"

"None that I could find. I thought maybe it was because I hadn't found the others, you know, people with North or South America, or maybe the west coast of Africa on their faces. I spent months scanning people at the mall, to no avail. And then my older sister hit puberty."

"And stole your superpowers?" He sounds oddly fascinated.

"No. But she cried a lot. The drama in our house went up by like a thousand percent. It was more fun watching Ashley get into trouble for trying to sneak out to meet boys."

"So that's where you get it from?"

I curl into him, laughing. "Maybe, but watch it because she's a police officer now."

Burke

I should be a gentleman at this point and return her drone before escorting Cassidy back to her tent. But I don't want to. I'm having fun talking to her in the dark, like a grown-up slumber party, and I don't mind the way her body is tucked against mine in the slightest. I fucking love it. She smells sweet with a hint of spice and something I can't quite place that's absolutely intoxicating.

And I know without a shadow of a doubt that she's absolutely gorgeous, every inch of her. But she's not ready to hear that from me yet. She'll see it as trying too hard, even if I mean every word, so I bite my tongue and concentrate on making her laugh. I know she's going to tell me she needs to leave soon, but I'm stringing this out as long as I can manage.

I stay silent for a long moment when she finally says softly, "Burke, I need to get back. Seriously. Can you give me back Betsy?"

"You named it Betsy? Somehow that fits."

"I did."

"Will you promise not to send Betsy or yourself into any strangers' tents?"

"I'll promise to stick to the job I was assigned, how's that?"

I growl as I slowly lever myself up from Cassidy's warmth. "When can I see you again?"

"Burke…"

"Cassidy. I'm not leaving this thing between us without a fight."

"I don't know, okay? I've got a lot on my plate with this new job. I doubt you live anywhere near me, and maybe we should leave it on a high note?" She sounds unsure and I concur. That sounds like a bad idea to me. I'm about to turn on a lantern to get the process of returning to normal started when my phone buzzes like the world's coming to an end. I bend over to grab it from the pile by the top of the cot. There's about six text messages with alert signs. I scroll through them as fast as I can. I hear Cassidy's phone ping repeatedly, too.

We're to stay in position, lights out until Security comes through with a roll call followed by an all-clear. Nobody is to be out of shelter and live ammunition can be expected by anyone roaming around. Fuck.

"You get anything more than stay put?" I ask Cassidy. I doubt she'd get more detail than me given I don't think she has more than a minimum security clearance but you never know.

"No. Stay where you are until told otherwise, basically."

"Hmm. Let's move to the other cot and leave this

one where any visitors will have to trip over it."

I hear her gulp. "Do you think it's something bad?"

"I don't know, princess, but they wouldn't be threatening live rounds if it wasn't serious. And we're pretty far removed out here which could be a good thing or a not so good thing."

"I don't suppose you have a gun?"

"No, but I've got a fairly wicked knife that can do plenty of damage if necessary."

"Alright, well this is your space so just tell me where to go."

Since I'm already up, I set about arranging the minimal furniture in a way that we can stay comfortable and any intruders can't maneuver. Then I guide her over to me with the penlight. This time settling her against my chest. My knife is strapped to my thigh and the rest of it is just waiting to see if we can learn more.

"I could send Betsy up, she's got night vision cameras."

"Too dangerous, Cass. I know she's small, but it could still be enough to call attention to us. Same with talking. We should keep it quiet until we know what's going on."

She nods against my chest and I give in to the temptation to simply touch her. Rubbing small circles on her back until I feel her relax against me. Well, as much as she can, anyway. Her spine is still tight, ready to jump at any moment.

It's a long wait and Cassidy is finally asleep when there's a loud knock on the door before it pushes open and a high beam LED flashlight shines in my face, pretty much blinding me. "Security — Jamieson, right?"

"Yeah. Security who, for the record?"

"Carlyle. Who's your friend?" Thankfully he moves the flashlight away from shining in her eyes.

Fuck, I don't know Cassidy's last name. That won't come across so great. But without hesitation she brings her head up, rubbing her eyes. "I'm Cassidy Van Houen. What's going on?"

That's my girl, no pussyfooting around.

"Briefing at 0800 tomorrow. They'll let everyone know what they need to know then. No wandering around tonight though, got it? We've got to keep the perimeter clear."

I can see Cassidy narrow her eyes at him, but she nods and watches as the guy in full military gear turns to leave.

"So roomie, looks like you're stuck with me," Cassidy says with a yawn.

"Dream come true, princess. You ready to get

some real shut-eye? I can bring the other cot over or you can curl up with me. I know which one I'd prefer but I'll let you pick."

"Gee, how generous of you. Actually, Burke, while it might not be wise I feel safer sticking close to you so…"

"Done." I'm not going to argue with a woman who's offering up exactly what I want. Okay, maybe it's not everything I want, but for right this minute I'm good.

"Come on, then." I scoot down until I'm lying flat and tuck Cassidy up against my side. She's really not very big, and with her head on my shoulder I wrap around her, pulling the one blanket up so it's mostly covering her shoulders and feet. "Umm," she murmurs contently as she relaxes, and I press one kiss onto the top of her head. It's all I'm allowing myself because otherwise I might not stop. I can feel her lose the tension in her shoulders as she falls asleep again. I don't dare move for fear of disturbing her so I keep still, thinking about how fast life can change when you aren't expecting it.

Cassidy

Mmm. I come awake with a smile, my eyes still closed. It's that delicious feeling when you wake up naturally on a Saturday morning looking forward to the day and with no particular place to be. I try to roll over and stretch into that feeling, but something's blocking me. Something big and warm. Oh.

I hold my breath while opening my eyes and adjusting to what I've just remembered. Burke. Only now I get to see him in person in the daylight. Is he still asleep? Nope, those warm amber eyes are watching me now with amusement.

It's a little surreal actually seeing him after spending the night together in the dark. It hardly seems possible, but he's even better looking in person. His hair is mussed as if he's run his fingers through it and he has a slight crease in his right cheek (he'll kill me if I call it a dimple) that I hadn't noticed before.

"Morning, princess."

I slant an annoyed mock glare at him. "Why do you keep calling me princess? You should know by now that shoe definitely doesn't fit."

"But it does. You're gorgeous, Cass. And you make me laugh. I was just waiting here last night for you to come in and surprise me with a kiss. Finally break the curse."

I grimace, realizing just how muddy my mouth feels after not brushing my teeth last night. "That would be more of a punishment right now. I don't suppose you have any way to brush your teeth way out here?"

"Bottle of water and a toothbrush." He shrugs slightly. As sweet and gorgeous as he is, I'm not ready to share a toothbrush. Somehow that seems more intimate than sex. Which is crazy, I know.

His hands curve around my waist and then suddenly he's tickling me, gently but with purpose. I convulse while shrieking, "Burke!" His touch softens, and he starts dropping teasing kisses on my neck and shoulder. "Fine, I'll do all the kissing. Sure you don't want to add Madagascar this morning?"

I consider it, I really do. Particularly since I can feel his cock hard against my thigh, and parts of me are more than interested in exploring that further. But… we have to be in the company of a lot of other people soon, and a love bite, even one that completes the map on my face, might give the wrong impression. Equally possible absolutely nobody would notice but… "Raincheck?" I ask softly.

"Sure, baby. Like I said, whenever you're ready. Might as well get up though, eh?"

He jackknifes off the cot and I take a moment to appreciate the size of the bulge, now at eye level. Good thing those sleep pants of his are loose. I really should put a stop to anything developing further between us. I can't see how it could go anywhere and I'm not going to have any spare time to give to a long-distance relationship for at least the next couple of years. But he's so adorable, standing there smiling down at me. I don't have the heart to put up that wall right now.

"Um, where's the bathroom?" I inquire prosaically as I push myself up to standing.

He gestures grandly at the tent door. "Wherever you like."

"You mean?"

He nods. "Ever been camping?"

"Not the kind that didn't have restroom facilities."

"Well, guys definitely have it easier in that department. Just point that cute tush downhill and you'll be fine. Consider it another growth experience."

I roll my eyes. Looks like someone was paying

attention to all the personal development jabber they were going on about a few days ago. I don't really want to discuss how to potty in the woods so I head outside with the small roll of toilet paper Burke hands me, determined to figure this out for myself. It shouldn't be that strange, right? Humans have been relieving themselves for millions of years without the benefits of indoor plumbing.

As soon as I lower my pants, I've got a mosquito bite on my ass. Fuck. I go as fast as I can, determined to send my plumber an extra large gift basket for Christmas this year when I'm safely back in the city. I've been taking him for granted — he deserves to know about my newfound respect.

When I go back to the tent, Burke is brushing his teeth just as he described right outside of the tent. He spits and hands me the water bottle. I rinse my mouth and hands as best I can and then he carefully hands me Betsy. I sigh with relief when I see she's okay. Her batteries are run down, but I can fix that easily enough back at the main tent.

We walk towards the center of the compound a few minutes early. I was hoping to get a shower and breakfast but it's looking like I'm going to have to choose between them. At the moment, my stomach is winning. It's weird that the war games have set hours of operation, but I guess it makes sense. It would be too complicated to set up separate kitchens for the two opposing sides plus all the operational staff. In any event, on normal days, 'warfare' starts at 8 am but it sounds like today that's been pushed off to thirty minutes after whenever the briefing ends. So for now, everyone is mingling and chatting and not worried about being killed.

Despite his words to the contrary, I'm half expecting Burke to split off and go find his peers. I'm still not sure exactly what he's doing here or what he does for a living, but now's not the time to ask. I have a feeling the busy-ness of the next two weeks will have us drifting apart until all we're doing is giving each other a friendly wave from a distance. It makes me a little sad just thinking about it, but I like to be mentally prepared.

We walk towards the mess hall tent, which is huge but mostly a sea of folding cafeteria tables which remind me of high school and the complex politics of seating arrangements. Too close to the cheerleaders and you were a hanger-on. Too close to the jocks and well, might as well be wearing that red A.

This time though I'm amused because people are trying to hide their smiles, well most of them. I see Violet off to one side with a big grin on her face. I can't figure it out until a long arm reaches over me and puts the plate of bacon and scrambled eggs I was eyeing on my tray. Oh. He's hovering. That's a first. I can't hold back the smile when I look up at him. But he's busy reaching to the back of the setup for a small bowl of strawberries. That goes on my tray too. "Burke? What are you doing?"

"Making sure you eat properly. They always put the oldest stuff up front. Why? You allergic to anything?"

"No." I shake my head, still smiling. "Thanks," I add belatedly, because I'm still bemused by his protectiveness. He hasn't put anything on his own tray yet. I scan the tent, wondering if there are any power stations in here. Eventually I spot one that's not already in use over on one big table to the side. It's occupied on one end but not the other, so I head that way with my tray. I want to get Betsy charged up while I have the chance.

I get Betsy all squared away, her little lights blinking happily as she sucks up her energy breakfast. The idea that we're eating together makes me grin, but I frown when someone's curious finger reaches out to touch the little drone. Maybe this wasn't such a good idea. But that guy quickly retreats under the power of my glare and I use Burke's trick of an upended water glass to put up a no-touch zone around my baby.

Burke sits down next to me, the entire opposite end of the bench lifting under his weight and it's not like he's got any body fat.

"Eat, princess," He orders as if I've been waiting for him. I roll my eyes, but I'm too hungry to argue first and dig in. For mass-produced food it's not too bad, but maybe that's just my stomach talking. I have a feeling it's going to be a long day.

Burke

I'm fucked. I can feel Cassidy mentally pulling away but I swear it's the words in her head that are doing it and nothing specific to me. It's like she's telling herself I'm some kind of illusion and therefore I become one. And no, I'm not generally that philosophical, but where am I going to find another Cass? I need to hang on to this one, if she'll let me. And just to be clear, she really is gorgeous. Her hair is the same color as the ground cinnamon my mother is always putting in everything. And she has this little spray of matching freckles across her nose. Not to mention the most kissable lips I've ever seen, which is why I'm confounded as to how I haven't kissed them yet. I need her to relax about us enough for me to get a taste of those lips asap.

Then there's the whole thing brewing here on the island. That's another big obstacle getting in the way of me spending time with Cass. I'm hearing bits and pieces of chatter and none of it is good. If I had my way, she'd be on the first large boat out of here, but I doubt that's going to be possible any time in the next few days. Next best is Cass stays surrounded by other people she already knows and that means not staying with me because I can bet my annual salary I'll be required personnel at the shoreline. At least until the infiltrators are identified and located. I'm not so worried that Cassidy is going to argue about staying in my tent, I mean you should have seen her face when she experienced roughing it for one morning, but I am suspicious that will give her a lot more time to build walls. A lot of very high, well-thought out, logical walls.

I've never in my life had to figure out how to keep a woman's attention. I'm not saying they were all obsessed with me. (Although I'm not denying it either...) but I've always been upfront that there were no strings involved and when I moved on, I never bothered looking back.

Strings are definitely involved with Cass, have been ever since she got embarrassed via drone and I've never tried to tell her otherwise. I want her and all her quirky stories in my life. Like now. Well, after this shit is over, because I need her staying alive to be in my life for as long as possible.

She's frowning at me, probably because I'm glaring at her, thinking about bad guys getting their hands on her. "Sorry, Cass. Just thinking about what's up. Worried about you."

She frowns harder. "Well, I'm worried about you, Burke. Let's go find out what they have to say. Knowledge is power and all that shit."

Cass is naïve as fuck if she thinks they're going to say anything of substance in this supposed 'briefing'. The real intel will be for need to know only and something tells me neither of us qualifies. But I amble behind her making sure any and all who see us together know she's with me. When we sit down in the tiny folding chairs, I stretch my arm out behind her shoulders. I'm not even trying to hide my intentions here, so I'm not too surprised when she rolls her eyes at me like I'm being a doofus. Don't care. I notice she doesn't move away, though. Score one for me.

As I expected, they blather on about unexpected events and an opportunity to practice personal safety protocol. I glance down at Cass to see her frowning in confusion. "They just mean the same old stuff that they send out every year about not parking in a dark corner."

She flicks her eyes my way briefly before whispering back, "That doesn't require live ammunition. What's going on?" She sounds like she's asking the guy with the microphone more than me, so I shut up.

Twenty minutes later we're no wiser but have been buried under a host of rules about not wandering around by yourself in the dark. Or by yourself in the woods. Since the big objective of the games is to capture the airstrip, which is open and in the middle I don't see that anyone is likely to change how they go about things. And they didn't say anything about being alone at the beach so clearly they're not worried about me.

Cass, on the other hand, has picked up on that and as we stand and start shuffling out of the tent pulls me aside with a firm grip on my arm. "Do they know you're out in that tent by yourself?"

I nod and take her hand to pull her towards the door.

"Burke, but that's dangerous."

"Princess, that little speech was for the benefit of all the civilians. They know all of us ex-military can handle ourselves. I've got my phone and a backup radio. I know how to subdue a panicked swimmer and I can definitely defend myself in less friendly situations. I'll be fine."

Cass bites the corner of her lip as she considers this, watching my face carefully. I give her an open smile and drop a kiss on her forehead to make her mad. It works.

Her concern turns to a glare, and she throws up her hands while walking towards one of the admin tents, Betsy clutched carefully in one hand. I let her go. I don't want to, because I can already sense that I've got a lot of work to do convincing her to take a long-term chance on me. But I want her safe and in large groups and I can't do that if I keep her with me. I watch her shapely backside disappear into the tent and then look around for who can tell me what's really going on.

Davis is headed towards the control tower. I jog in his direction until I'm within hailing distance.

"Yo, Davis!"

He turns and waits for me, grinning. "Heard you found looove last night."

"Knock it off, Davis. I found my future wife last night. I just need to convince her."

Now he's outright laughing and I don't even care. "What the fuck is going on, man?"

The hardened military guy eventually emerges from the joking pal as he sobers up. "Nobody knows much yet. A military-grade inflatable was found on the northwest beach last night. No insignia and no evidence of who was on board. Whoever it is has disappeared for the moment."

"But it's an island."

"Exactly, but we don't know if they came for us or didn't know we'd be here. The analysts are combing through the channels looking for any clues but apparently it's complicated by the fact this island keeps changing names."

"Since when have the bad guys ever called anything by the proper name?" I'm exasperated. They should know by now the who, what, and where of what's going on. I'll allow them another day or so to figure out the why. Of course, I'm not in charge of any of this shit so nobody cares — including Davis.

"That's all I know. You figure it out, drop me a hint." He turns back towards the squat tower.

Fuck. Okay, well, I know a little more than I did, and it confirms my instinct to get Cassidy away from the beach.

5

★ ★ ★

Cassidy

That man is so annoying! How am I ever going to successfully manage a team of guys just like him? Because you know they'll be just as cocky, if not worse. Even if I don't have any work authority over Burke, I've got the kind that comes from common sense that says a man by himself armed only with a knife is no match for two or more bad guys that probably have guns.

It bothers me all morning as I run drone patrols with my team. We haven't worked up to anything very exciting yet. Some of them can't even steer a straight course which is causing everyone else to stop and try to help. I take a few minutes to zip through one of the command tents, practicing snapping pics as I fly. I want to check and see if they're still legible or if the drone has to be stationary for that. It's just a quick fly through and there's not even any interesting documents out but for test purposes it's fine. And it leaves me plenty of time to stew about Burke.

Who should not be staying alone in that tent. But if I make a point of that to anyone in charge, I'll look like I care for personal reasons. And it's highly likely they won't take it seriously, which will just get me labeled as an overly anxious female — bring on the condescending 'don't worry about it, little girl' talk. So instead I make an executive decision.

"I'm going to work from my tent this afternoon — see if it improves the lag time." I announce just before we break for lunch. I get a few curious looks and some weak nods, but nobody challenges my completely made up explanation. We don't have a problem with lag time. Which is good, because I'm not going to be working from my tent either.

I head that way though and pack up my one duffel bag with my clothes and personal stuff, which doesn't amount to much. Then I go and grab lunch but instead of going through the line I duck my head into the kitchen and ask ever so sweetly if someone can wrap up some sandwiches so I can make sure my friend gets a chance to eat. The older wizened cook barking orders at his subordinates gives me a long look before winking at me. Then he shouts more orders at the young guys rushing around looking like they never should have volunteered for what they thought was an easy job. Moments later, Antonio, as he introduces himself, hands me a plastic canvas bag loaded with sandwiches, fruit, and some potato salad and even a few brownies. "Make sure he treats you right. Make him earn those brownies, Missy."

I grin at that, not sure if we're talking about the same activities that are brownie worthy. But I thank him and swing back by my tent, or at least it was my tent, and grab my duffel before lugging everything towards the beach. It takes considerably longer than my first nighttime foray because the luggage keeps swinging and hitting me on the ass, which makes it hard to walk. And the bag Antonio packed is getting seriously heavy. I'm contemplating stopping and eating some of it to lighten the load when I finally catch the glimmer of water. Not far now.

The tent is empty but I can tell Burke has been back because the furniture is in a more traditional arrangement, what little there is of it. I drop my bag on the unmade cot and take the food out towards the beach, wondering where the most annoying but cute man on the planet has wandered off to. I spot him way down at the end of the shore before the little spit staring off towards the horizon. It's too far and too windy to yell and hope he hears me, so instead I sit down on a large driftwood log and take out my controller for Betsy. She's still back at the working tent, sitting on my mini desk. With a few flicks of the toggle, I call her to me and she whirs into view in almost no time at all. How did I ever survive without one of these things?

I paw through the bag of food, looking for the perfect surprise that's not too heavy for Betsy to handle. It takes a minute, but down at the bottom next to the brownies is a little plastic container of strawberries. Perfect.

Betsy isn't really built for carrying capacity, but she does have one tiny set of pincers. It takes me another few minutes to figure out which toggles and buttons operate them but Burke still hasn't noticed me. Not exactly confidence building that he can handle bad guys on his own, is it? So I get Betsy to pick up the strawberry and zoom her down the shoreline, up fairly high because I want to see if I can surprise Burke. I must have, because he whips around when I drop the strawberry on his head. I wave to catch his attention, and he starts loping down the beach.

I think my ovaries explode at that sight because that much man moving like he owns the ground he's covering? Just yum. Maybe I'll ask him to do ten laps before I bring out the brownies. For his health, you know?

Except he's frowning heavily when he arrives in front of me. And damn him, he's not even breathing hard. "Cass? What the hell are you doing here?"

Okaaay, did I completely misunderstand something? "Err, I brought lunch. I can take it back." I start to stand, but a heavy hand on my shoulder keeps me down.

"Fuck it, Cass. No wandering about on your own.

I thought you understood that part." He's practically growling, his biceps bulging as his fists clench.

"You're wandering about on your own."

"That's different."

"How? Because I'm a woman?"

"No. Because you're a woman that hasn't had any training in hand to hand combat. And because you're my woman and I don't want you getting hurt!" He's down in my face now and I'm so surprised by his bluster and the outright claim that I sort of knew he felt but really hadn't expected him to say that I do the first thing that occurs to me. I wrap my hands around his neck and pull him close enough to kiss.

I can tell he didn't expect that, but it doesn't take him long to adjust, and suddenly he's picking me up, my legs naturally curving around his waist. He wastes no time letting me know he's bigger and stronger, as his tongue ravishes my mouth while his hands palm my ass, his fingers digging in to anchor me against his growing erection. I grind myself against him, eager to get closer, needing to feed the empty ache between my thighs.

I'm almost there, the curl of need spiraling tighter in my belly when he pulls back. "Cassidy? Are you trying to distract me? If you get yourself seriously injured so help me I'll redden that ass until you have to stay in one place for a month." He lightly swats my rear with one hand and the combination of his touch and the way it pushes me even tighter against his cock sends me over the edge. My head falls back, and some kind of weird gurgle emerges from my throat. I don't care, I'm too busy blushing as my pussy spasms against him, wetness soaking through my shorts as I cum in his arms.

Slowly, and with caution, I open my eyes and look straight into the knowing gaze of Burke. He's smirking a little, and it just makes him look even more delectable.

"Next time you do that, I'm going to be inside you. Understand?"

I blink. "For the record, I was not the distraction." I say wryly, and he grins.

"Princess, nothing a man likes to hear more than that his woman finds him irresistible."

Since I can't reach his rear, I tug on his ear until he slowly lowers me to my feet. He doesn't let me go far, though. Those amazingly long arms of his cage me in a small circle that I find oddly endearing.

I need to regain my sense of authority. I'm sure Burke would argue that I never had any to begin with, but I felt like I did and that's all I'm going for. Bracing my hands on my hips I stare up at him. "I'll go be with other people when you do, got it?"

"Like hell you will." He growls instinctively before looking a bit sheepish. "Oh, that. I thought you meant…"

I swat his arm. "Grow up, Burke."

"Baby, if you couldn't tell…"

I chase him down the beach, or rather he lets me run after him before swinging me close, my back to his front and his arms criss-crossed over my chest. He leans down to nuzzle my ear. "Cass, let's be real clear with each other. I don't touch other women and you don't go near another man romantically. You find yourself in trouble up to your ears I expect you to let the nearest friendly swing you over his shoulder to get you out of there. But I don't want you anywhere near trouble. Hence the request to stay with the crowd. Now are you going to do that for me?"

I stare out at the horizon, empty and calm, no sign of the potential threat lurking anywhere. "No," I respond calmly. "Not without you. You think you're invincible and you're not. So Betsy and I are staying here with you. My stuff is already in the tent. Now why don't we eat?"

"Anybody hearing you, babe, would think you were suggesting a threesome." He sounds appalled at the idea, and I giggle. Something tells me this conservative streak is a new discovery for Burke and I'm going to enjoy watching it unfold. I think. I sure had fun a few minutes ago.

Burke

This little tent has never looked as flimsy as it does now, in the broad light of day now that we have some idea of what's going on. Seeing Cass perched on the end of the cot, her brown eyes sparkling with challenge, has me wanting to tackle her and put her somewhere safe. She's made it clear that's not going to work so instead I study the layout trying to figure out how to make anyone coming in go for me first.

Silently I motion Cass up. When she reluctantly stands with her eyebrows practically shouting questions, I push the two cots together and lash the frames with the one and only belt I brought with me. I'm not even sure why, because I never wear the fucking things. Then I make up the now almost double bed, those cots are damn narrow, doing my best to avoid a crevassing seam in the middle. When I have it to my satisfaction I turn to find my girl practically shooting sparks. "Aren't you making a lot of assumptions, big guy?"

"The only assumption I'm making is that I'm going to be between you and anyone coming in here. The best way I see to accomplish that in a tent is to have you under me. Anything else happening is open for discussion. But I'll reiterate my earlier statement. The next time you cum, you'll be doing it around my cock so…"

She blushes, and it's adorable. I don't care if it takes two years for her to accept how badly I want her. She's worth the wait, and I never thought I'd say that about anyone. I take pity on her because I'm really not trying to make her uncomfortable. "Come on, now that's done why don't you show me what Betsy can do?"

"Really?" Her face lights up and I see her inner geek shine through. Suddenly I'm picturing a little girl with pigtails and big glasses and a little lab coat. Why I don't know, but out of nowhere I want that. More than anything. A little girl, smart as her momma. A family. My mother would be laughing her head off if she could hear the thoughts racing through my head. She's bitten her lips more times than I can count when someone else brings up the subject of grandchildren. Mom always said she never wanted to pressure me, but I felt the unsaid words, anyway. She's gonna love Cassidy. Assuming I can convince my girl to give me a chance beyond this week. And that is going to take more than making her cum fast and hard. That just gets me an interview, proving I'm the man for the permanent job requires a lot more.

I tug her behind me out to the beach again. The remains of our picnic neatly packed up and waiting by the log we used as a table. I learn more about drones in the next thirty minutes than I ever really wanted to, but I'm having the time of my life watching the emotions flit across Cassidy's expressive face.

She's bright and vivid and her whole body moves with her feelings.

Right now she's quiet, staring out over the water after Betsy when I decide to do a little probing. "So other than being a superhero, what did you dream about when you were little?"

"You mean besides being taller than all my siblings?"

"Yeah, the long-term personal goals. Princess firefighter, or CEO boss lady?"

"Damn, I didn't know you could be a firefighter and a princess. Where were you when they were doing career counseling?"

"I can't take credit, that was my mini cousin Anna's idea."

"Mini cousin?"

"Second removed or whatever? She's my cousin Daniel's daughter. Mini cousin fits the bill." I shrug, she's trying to change the subject and I want to know if she dreamed about weddings and babies. I know. How the mighty have fallen. Only took one quirky girl with bright eyes and a partial map of Africa on her face to bring me to my knees.

"Hey, Betsy's batteries are getting low. Want to come with me to go charge them up?"

Shit. I'm supposed to stay here until five, but on the other hand, not much is happening. "Hang on, let me just check in and then we should be able to go.”

I quickly text Pablo, who agrees to take a few hours of my shift in exchange for the early part of his. Works for me because then I have an excuse to spend sunset with my girl at the beach.

“Okay, let’s go. Pablo’s on his way.”

“Who is this mysterious Pablo?”

“Nobody. Absolutely nobody.” Only the Don Juan of the sixth fleet to hear him tell it. No way I’m letting him show off his pearly whites to Cass. I hustle her down the path towards the main event, and sure enough, Pablo is coming our way. I wave and keep going maybe a little too fast because Cass is laughing. “Where’s the fire?”

I slow down now that we’re past having to spend time chit chatting. “Sorry, princess. Hey, you never did tell me about your big dreams.”

She’s looking up at me quizzically. “Changing the subject is not going to work, big guy. What’s got you so hot under the collar?”

I sigh and confess, “He’s the worst flirt, I didn’t want you to have to listen to him lay out his catalog of lines.”

Her jaw drops a little and she sort of shakes her head like she’s trying to wake up. “I think I like your world view, Burke. I might have to move there.”

I don't have a chance to ask her what she means because we're in the community zone now and people are coming and going more actively. In theory they should all be out attempting to 'kill' each other, but it seems like that's taking second priority to people's need to gossip and commiserate.

Two women are talking behind us, loudly, but it takes a second for their words to sink in. "Oh my God, I can't believe he's with her. I mean, how does he get it up looking at that face?"

"Well, she probably lets him do whatever from behind, you know?"

Fuck, I start to turn around ready for the first time in my life to hit a woman, but Cassidy has a firm grip on my arm. "Don't, Burke. If you didn't figure it out, they want your attention. Don't give it to them."

"But those bitches…"

"Are exactly that. Trust me, I'm not really that generous, but after years of that shit in high school I finally figured out that they go for whatever's obvious. They don't even want to work hard to insult someone. My face is obvious. But if it wasn't, they'd be saying something about my weight. Or my boobs."

"You could stand to put on a few more pounds, but I'm not complaining. Your boobs are fucking perfect. And so is your face. Well, at least it would be if you'd let me add Madagascar." I wrap my arm around her shoulders to bring her close against my side. If she won't let me tell off the bitch brigade, I need to touch her.

She snort laughs. "Fine. You can do that tonight before bed. Happy?"

I groan because just the thought of marking her as mine before curling up together in our makeshift bed has my cock pressing painfully against my fly. And now I've got to wait for hours. Fine, maybe it's like three before I can get her alone again, but still.

And I'm not forgetting about the two women behind us. As we head into the dining tent, I take a brief backward glance to register their faces. I'll find a way to make sure they don't spread that kind of nasty somehow. Or at the very least ensure they have to spend a lot of time downwind of the portable toilets.

6

Cassidy

Burke is a genuinely good guy, even if he is a bit annoying with his bossy commands. And while I'm sure he's not completely naïve about the baser side of human nature, I'm not sure he realizes how often it pops up in everyday civilian life. I'm trying to force myself to relax, worry about only what I can control and not try to anticipate our eventual breakup. I haven't even known the guy forty-eight hours. That's a little early to either be in love or be sure it won't work. I think I've done both. Fuck.

And why is it guys get to just float through all this emotional shit? Burke doesn't look worried at all. While Betsy charges, I sip on a soda and finally just blurt it out, "How on earth do you think we can be anything more than a working vacation fling?"

He frowns at me, like the question offends him, but he takes his time formulating his answer. "Because there's nothing about you that's ordinary, princess.

And a weekend hookup would be ordinary in the extreme. If I have to chase you around the world to convince you, I'll do it. You can't shake me that easily."

"But…"

"Stop overthinking it, Cass. I don't want you feeling pressured to do anything you're not ready for. Scared of maybe, yes. But nothing that feels truly wrong. Got it? There's no deadline. Just because we're here together for two weeks doesn't mean jack shit."

"It doesn't?" I'm fascinated.

"Not really. Remember, I told you about all those potential endorsements that wanted me to change things?"

"Yeah?"

"Those were just the really big ones. I had about five years of small to medium shit and while it wasn't a lot of cash at the time, my parents made me invest it. And I've never spent it."

"What are you trying to tell me?"

"That I'm not a billionaire but I can afford to quit my job and chase after you for a few years and if that's what it takes I'll do it without second thoughts."

"Oh." For some reason, that puts a big smile on my face that I can't quite seem to lose. Maybe it's the ridiculousness of it all. Or maybe it's because his eyes are blazing with conviction and he's cute and hot and sweet all at once.

I still don't think he can be that sure so fast, but I kind of like that he thinks he can. And maybe I owe it to myself to not shut him down completely. Just a little common sense but lose the negativity. My sister would tell me to jump his bones, but then she has a lot more experience with handcuffs. My brothers would try to convince me to take a ten-year vow of celibacy just to see if he'll wait it out that long. And then they would take bets. For no particular reason except they like to boss me around. And they think I'm still six.

My brain is tired. Between thinking about possible bad guys and whatever this is with Burke, plus learning how to maneuver Betsy, I'm feeling pretty done for the day. Consequently, I don't protest when Burke leads me out of the dining tent an hour later and back towards the beach.

We're just in time for the early glimmers of sunset. And the wind has picked up so I'm a bit chilly but before I can suggest going to the little tent to grab my sweatshirt I'm engulfed in warm man. For once I let myself relax into this. Whatever the hell it is. Because it just feels so good. Silently we watch the sun slip down behind the gentle waves, the colors deepen and brighten in the sky above with sizzling streaks of coral and I sigh at the beauty of it all.

And then I'm gasping because warm lips are

kissing the back of my neck, somehow finding nerve endings that fire up my entire body. Instinctively, I tilt my head to give him better access, and he takes full advantage.

"My girl, Cassidy. Tell me you're my girl." His kisses tease that spot right behind my ear.

"Mmm," is all I can manage. My hands grip his arms wrapped firmly around my middle.

His teeth scrape gently against my earlobe. "I'm not letting you go, princess. Not until you say it." He's teasing but there's a thread of steel in there beneath that. I ponder what he's asking. Really asking.

"I'm certainly not anybody else's," I finally say.

He laughs and I feel it all down my back. "Smart and stubborn. You really are my girl."

Burke pulls me in, angling me against his right shoulder, and then I feel his lips kiss just under my jawline. "Marking you now, babe. Everyone is going to know you're mine from here on out." He sucks hard on that spot, and the sensation travels all the way down to my clit, which throbs in response. My legs move restlessly over his, but he holds me tight, still intent on making sure I never forget this moment. I won't, I promise. Because it's so much more than a love bite, it's humor and caring and understanding me at a level most people don't even make an effort to get to.

He rubs his thumb gently over the small patch of skin before shifting my weight back to center, resting his chin on the top of my head.

The dark is closing in and reluctantly I push myself up from Burke's lap. He lets me this time, and together we take the short path to the tent, which looks small and forlorn on the short bluff overlooking the beach. I feel limp like a noodle but not unhappy. Just a bit overwhelmed. I stare down at the bed Burke constructed earlier while he turns on a small lantern.

"You want me to step out while you change?" he asks gently.

One more thing to think about. "I'm too tired to care. Suit yourself."

His snort is followed by a soft laugh. "Well, that put me in my place, didn't it?" He drops a swift kiss on my head and steps out, anyway. I find my pj's and strip down, then remember I haven't brushed my teeth so once I'm covered again I go in search of a bottle of water and step outside. Burke is standing there, hands on his hips, looking thoughtful. He turns when he hears me open the door.

"Ready?"

"Just need to brush my teeth and um, use the facilities."

At that, he frowns. "I don't want you wandering

too far from the tent, okay? Can you manage in that clump of bushes right there?" He points and I nod. I can't believe I've come to the point of discussing bathroom arrangements with a man I barely know. Twice in one day.

Of course Burke waits for me. It's a good thing I grew up with brothers and don't have a shy bladder. But I'm certainly not feeling sexy by the time I wash my hands with the bottled water and head into the tent for the next challenge, sleeping in the same bed. But this time without the sense of immediate panic that smoothed over the awkwardness last night.

I crawl under the covers and immediately close my eyes.

Burke laughs when he comes back in. "Maybe I should start calling you possum. Scoot over for a second so I can get in. Then you can have more space."

I do, keeping my eyes sealed shut. I didn't ask if he was going to wear pajamas and I sort of assumed he would, but now I don't know. I don't dare risk visual confirmation at this point.

Burke

If someone had told me the smart girls were this much fun in high school, I might still be a virgin, but

I'd have enjoyed those years a lot more. Cassidy is going out of her way to not-so-subtly let me know nothing is happening tonight. I already knew that but I'm taking it as a good sign because it means she's thinking about it. A truly disinterested woman would be well, I'm not entirely sure, but it's not what Cass is doing.

I'm both looking forward and dreading having her soft curves under me all night, but I'm still sure this is the best plan under the circumstances. I roll onto my side so I can essentially lean over her with my back to the door and not crush her so she can't breathe. That would kind of defeat the purpose of protecting her. Gravity pulls her into the dent of the mattress made by my heavier body, so she's right up against me. She fits perfectly.

She sighs softly, mumbles something unintelligible, and finally relaxes. I don't dare start kissing her, so I settle for breathing in her delicate scent. It's not flowers but something spicier, just like Cass.

At some point in the night she rolls over because I wake up to find her spooning me in tight formation, her perfectly curved ass cupping my morning erection in a way that has me afraid to move. But in a good way. Except she might not speak to me again if I spray cum all over her pajamas before she's even fully awake. She stirs and I groan as my cock starts thinking it's about to get really lucky.

"Burke?" she mumbles, confused.

"Careful how you move there, princess. Things are a bit... delicate."

She freezes, and I can practically feel her brain taking inventory. "Oh." Her giggle is soft and sweet.

Instead of sliding away, she gives a little wiggle that has me seeing stars. "Fuck," comes out as grunt because I'm having to bite my lip to try to regain some control.

"Do you want me to get up?" Her voice is innocent and curious.

"That depends on whether you want my cum all over you. If you don't, I'd suggest exiting — carefully — in the next five seconds."

"Oh, er, um." She slides away carefully but instead of getting out of bed, sits up and looks down at me. "So how does that work, exactly?"

My eyes fly to hers in disbelief.

She grins. "I'm so glad I'm not a guy. I meant the covering me in your cum part. Do you like direct it like a garden hose? I've always wondered, and it would be weird to ask my brothers. Ick."

I have questions. Lots of questions, but my brain can only deal with the image of shooting my load all over her soft skin. "Come here, little girl." I leer at Cass. I'm 99% sure she's going to evacuate. And I'm right.

She slides off the far side of the bed with a big smile. "No way. I'm on to you." She stands there fiddling with the tie of her pajama bottoms, staring at my cock that's begun to weep, probably through the light pants I wore for Cassidy's benefit. If I had to guess, she's probably staring at a wet spot, but I'm too far gone to care.

But if I don't get up, housekeeping is going to have a big chore, and it so happens that I'm the sole employee of housekeeping for this tent. I get up with a mighty groan because I'm old and deprived.

"Stay here," I growl at Cass, mostly because I want to slam her back down on the bed and sink into her warm depths. Instead I head out of the makeshift building and over to the nearest tree where I can keep an eye on the tent and still take care of my most pressing issue.

When I feel like there's a modest chance I won't beg Cass to take pity on me, I head back inside. Not that I'm against begging, but I don't think this is the right time to put any pressure on her. As offensive as some might find it, once you have the fish on your hook you don't take anything for granted. But just so we're clear when it comes to Cassidy I've got my line in for permanent forevers. I'm smart enough not to mention that right now, too.

But when I pop open the flimsy door, she's frowning down at her phone, looking beyond perplexed.

"Princess?"

"Hmmm? I just got the strangest message. It's from an HR lady, says she needs to see me this morning before I start my shift. What on earth for?"

Something sours in my belly and all I can think of is the two bitches from yesterday. Making fake complaints to HR would be a new low but then they were pretty far down in the crap layer already from what I could see.

"Don't suppose you'll let me go with you?"

"To meet with HR? Hell, no." She gives me a half-hearted smile that shows her anxiety. "But thanks. I appreciate the offer."

I wasn't really expecting anything else from the woman that planned to be a superhero. That career path is pretty much for those that want to go off by themselves to save the world. Unless it's Batman of course, but I always thought Robin was more about an excuse to hear himself talk.

"How about this, then? We'll go get breakfast and I'll hang nearby, and if it has anything to do with the bitch brigade, you text me. Alright?"

"Oh, it couldn't have anything to do with them. How could it?" I see the naïve wheels in her head start turning. "Errr. Alright. Let's go. I'd like to get this over with."

I pull her close for a minute. This is new, the

nervous Cassidy although I can see how she's related to the shy version. I just want to make it all go away for her, but short of our impromptu plan, I can't think of anything else.

"Come on then. Now that you've got Madagascar your powers should be at full capacity."

Her hand flies to her neck and a look of shock comes over her pretty face. "Oh shit. I forgot. Will it look strange if I wear a scarf with this t-shirt? Do you have a scarf? Okay, that was a silly question. Maybe I can borrow one from someone." Her eyes dart around the tent as if looking for the imaginary fashion accessory, but I capture her hand and pull it down so I can drop kisses on the spot I claimed yesterday.

"Stop worrying, Cassidy. Nobody would dare notice. Let's go eat. You'll feel better with coffee."

7

Cassidy

What the hell does HR want with me? Particularly during the games which are pretty much an alpha male's fantasy of the perfect birthday party. I can't stop fussing about it even though I know perfectly well it won't change anything or put me in a more adept frame of mind. Burke does his best to distract me and he almost succeeds once or twice. But my stomach is still in knots when I get up from the bench seat in the dining hall slash mess and head over to the tent where I was told to find Missy Golman. I haven't got a clue who Missy is outside of being in HR but I guess we're about to find out.

There's no door, so I pull back the tent flap as slowly as possible, just in case she's with someone else. Huh. She's not, but somehow she looks like she spent two hours in front of a mirror with hot and cold running water and all the other amenities of civilized life. Maybe she's staying in a hotel.

"Hi. I'm Cassidy. You wanted to see me?"

"Oh hi, Cassidy. Yes. I did. Please have a seat." She continues going over her notes in her perfect pink and gold folder. I wait silently, letting my gaze rest just over her shoulder. If this is a test, I'm not letting down my guard.

"Okay." She smiles warmly as she closes the folder and sets it aside. "How are you finding the games so far, Cassidy?"

I shrug. That has to be a trick question. "Fine. No complaints."

"Err yes. Well, unfortunately someone has filed a complaint about you. That you were observed making unwelcome sexual advances to a male employee."

My eyes bug out. Not that I don't understand women are capable of harassing a man, just that I don't think I would ever have the nerve. "You're kidding, right?" This must be one of those prank things.

"I'm afraid not. There were actually two corroborating witnesses but even if there was just one we always take these matters extremely seriously."

Burke's fateful prediction rings in my ear. Two witnesses, huh? "Are you absolutely sure you're not talking about my boyfriend?" Burke will forgive that white lie I'm thinking.

"Oh. Well, um." She looks down over her notes. "I can't say for sure, but from the report that doesn't seem likely. We'll be interviewing everyone involved before we make any kind of determination."

"I'd like to clear this up right now, if you don't mind," I respond rather grimly. I take out my cellphone and queue up Burke's number. Thank God he thought to put it in for me yesterday.

Hey, guess what? You're now officially my boyfriend.

It's only a few seconds before his reply comes back. **Hot damn! On my way.**

I don't know how he knows where to go. I'm a little suspicious that he might have followed me, but I'm too grateful to see him stick his head in the tent with a bashful grin, charm on full throttle.

"Ma'am. Is my little princess in some kind of trouble?"

I choke in my attempt to keep my eyes from rolling back in my head. He's laying it on a little too thick. But apparently not because nobody is paying attention to me. Missy has stood up (something she didn't do for me) and is fangirling all over Burke. "Oh, you're Burke Jamieson! I didn't really believe it when..." She shuts her mouth abruptly. I can see from the ever so subtle tightening of Burke's eyes that he caught her slip. And he's not happy about it. But he keeps up the lazy charm. "One and the same, ma'am. Now about our Cassidy, here. I can't imagine she did anything wrong. I mean I've been with her pretty much twenty-four seven."

"And you're really in a relationship?" She sounds almost disappointed. "I mean, together?" Disbelief drips from her voice and Burke's goes to steel.

"If I had my way, she'd have my ring on her finger already. But Cassidy is old-fashioned and wants me to ask her daddy first. That doesn't mean that I take kindly to anyone implying I'm not serious about her or treating her with anything but the utmost respect." His warning is clear and Missy sits down abruptly.

"Oh, yes, of course. I'll be sure to clarify with the concerned parties." She doesn't sound like she's looking forward to that — at all.

"You do that." Burke gestures to me slightly, pulling me up from the metal folding chair that was teetering on one leg due to the uneven ground. "Any further unfounded accusations against either of us, and I'll be making a call to my Uncle Frank. Feel free to pass that on to the concerned parties as well." He nods abruptly and tugs me out of the tent. I'm bemused, but follow him out anyway. It's not like I want to spend more time chatting with Missy. When we're clear of the makeshift building, Burke pulls me into his arms and kisses me like the world is going to end in about ten minutes. When he reluctantly pulls back from my lips and I try to catch my breath he growls, "Fuck those bitches."

Well, I can't exactly disagree, but I suspect they're in for an unpleasant second meeting with Missy. She didn't strike me as someone that readily forgives being played for a fool. "Who's your Uncle Frank?" I ask instead, genuinely curious.

"Private Hollywood attorney," Burke grins down at me. "He always says he's not started the day right if he hasn't filed ten cease and desist orders before sitting down to breakfast."

Oh. Wow. Definitely a different world than my family. "You weren't really serious about talking to my father, were you?"

"Well, I am serious about marrying you and at some point that's going to involve talking to your father. I don't think I'd dare ask his permission though because odds are either you'd kill me or he'd turn me down so I prefer more of an ask for forgiveness plan, personally."

Wow. That's a lot to unpack. Way more than I was expecting. "I need to get to work." I chicken out. There's no other word for it.

"Stop worrying, princess. I'll be right here waiting." He gives me another brief kiss and then dares to pat my ass before sauntering towards one of the large tents I haven't been in yet. I stare after him, my jaw hanging down in bemusement.

"He is a fine-looking specimen, isn't he?"

I turn with fire in my eyes to see whose voice is oozing honey at my man only to find Violet, her green eyes laughing at me with glee. "Oooh, you've got it bad. Does he know?"

"He's too busy bossing me around and telling me we're getting married." I pout, I shouldn't. But I do.

Violet's smile turns a little sad at the corners. "Must be nice. I've practically stood on my head… No wait, I did that too once, trying to get one particular man to notice me. Nothing worked."

"Then he was an idiot," I say firmly. Any man should be lucky to have her want him. He might be exhausted, but lucky.

Violet's sigh is filled with longing. "Possibly. But a growly, gorgeous idiot. He's standing right over there if you want to see what floats my boat." She points into the shadows of an adjacent tent. There's a huge and fierce looking man lurking there. Considerably older than Violet, with his hands resting on his nearly non-existent hips, he's glaring at her like he's forcibly restraining himself from not flinging her over his shoulder.

"You sure he's not into you? I mean he's here, and he only has eyes for you so…."

"Really? Every time I look at him he's staring at the horizon line looking bored."

"Yeah, no." I correct her impression as clearly as I

can. Her expression turns mischievous, a new light dancing in her eyes as she sneaks a sideways peek at the glowering man.

"Someday I'm going to have my way with him." She licks her lips, and the man's glower deepens.

I'm suddenly hungry for popcorn and a comfy chair, but I have actual work to do. So I give a general wave in their direction which I don't think either of them notice and head off.

Cassidy

Daydreaming about a man and flying a drone don't really mix very well, if I'm honest. I catch myself, or rather Betsy, just in the nick of time before she slams into the broad trunk of a tree. It's weirdly caramel color with peeling red bark, so I think it's a madrona? Not really sure, but I'm positive it's going to take a crash with Betsy better than the little drone. I fly her away and into an open area while I catch my breath and promise her I'll focus more carefully.

I'm supposed to be tracking one of the demolition experts. Is it bad that I can't remember if he's ex-Marines or ex-Army? I mean I know *he* would think it was bad but honestly I can't keep track of these things and it's not like they're wearing insignia. One side is wearing orange armbands and the other blue, but they don't say Marines or Army. I know that sounds lame, but geez. Anyway, this guy who's laying a fake bomb under a truck at the moment is really boring. The bomb isn't, that's kind of fun. Obviously they don't want to really hurt anyone so they use these these remote controlled confetti bombs. I know, right? Only the confetti is dye-treated like stolen bank money, so anything it touches turns blue. Machinery, people, you name it. There's been more than one totally blue man at breakfast in the mess hall. Totally threw me the first time I saw it and now it just makes me giggle in sympathy.

So anyway, I'm tracking this guy and I'm a bit torn between doing my job and reporting the bomb to the side I'm supposed to be working for or sitting back and having a little excitement in an otherwise boring afternoon.

Alright, alright. I send the text to alert 'my side' to the bomb with the truck number. So, that was a little bit of fun watching from Betsy's camera as six men flee for their lives out of the nearby vehicles. They must really get razzed if they turn blue. I move Betsy out of the area just in case and fly her to my next target. I have a list of ten I'm supposed to check up on. It's a bit weird because they kept the drone team working together in one tent but divided us up between sides. I'm not entirely sure why except one or two of the women are still having trouble steering. And why is it only women on this team? Seems strange, but whatever. As long as nobody tries to get between me and my Betsy, we should be good. I check the time. I'm farther down my list than anyone else in the room, so I think I deserve a break.

By which I mean I steer Betsy towards the beach to check on Burke. I find him sitting on a log, staring out to sea with a pair of binoculars. His shirt is nowhere to be found, and he's only wearing brief swim trunks. I squirm in my seat because I want to be there, seeing if his skin tastes salty. I'll bet it does. Why didn't I find that out when I had the chance? Damn it. Just for fun, I bring Betsy down on top of his head. I can't see his reaction because her cameras don't face that way, but Betsy seems fine, so he must have figured it out. I know it when I hear his voice. "Cass? You swinging by just to say hi or did you need something?"

I fly the little drone up and down in front of his face. There, that's much better. I can't really tilt wings here or anything, so I settle for just hovering. I'm smiling, but it's not like he can see that.

"I'm taking that to mean you're just here to say hi. I wish it was the human you. Betsy's cute and all but I can't kiss her." He sounds forlorn, so I land Betsy down on his bare knee and turn off the rotors.

"Whatcha looking at, Cassidy?"

Oh fuck. I flip the camera off just as Tiffany comes up behind me. She's nice enough, but the worst gossip I've ever encountered, as in non-stop. She's not mean, she just chatters about anything and everything. Finding me staring at a screen full of naked man chest would be exciting enough for her to grab the mike in the mess hall at dinner.

"Just wrapping up a bomb siting, Tiff. You know how that blue dye gets everywhere?"

"Oh, um, sure." She doesn't sound convinced, but she's also lazy when it comes to acquiring information so she soon drifts over to Louisa who's attempting to infiltrate the command center of the opposing side.

Oh fuck, I just remembered Louisa's on the other side from me, so technically that's my command center. I guess I'd better get back to work. I bring Betsy back to life and spin a little circle in front of Burke to say goodbye before heading over to the air control tower to hide in plain site on the roof. I'll see Burke at dinner so I'd better keep my mind on the job until then.

Cassidy

Except Burke doesn't show up for dinner. He sends me a brief text just as I'm walking over to the mess tent.

Something came up. Don't come to the beach until you hear from me.

That has me frowning for all kinds of reasons and apparently stopping dead in my tracks too, since someone swears as they bump into me. I start walking again and gather some food on a tray while I try to figure out what's going on. Is Burke busy with work stuff or is something bad going down on the beach? And since when have I let myself get so distracted by a guy? This is not good. This is not how I want to prove myself to my new team or my bosses. Like a middle school girl waiting for a smile from the hot guy with a nearby locker.

But I can't just leave Burke to fare on his own. I know he's spent years doing that and he probably can take care of himself, but he wouldn't leave me to my own devices. At least I think he wouldn't? He's kind of doing that now.

I frown even harder into my bowl of chicken noodle soup until I hear a cheerful voice in front of me. "Is the soup really that bad? Or did it do something to make you mad?"

I glance up to see a woman standing with her own tray, holding a bowl of soup and wild blonde ringlets that cascade down onto the shoulders of her floral print dress. She's different. Not from regular people but she's definitely not ex-military, and she doesn't look like the ACI people either although there is quite a mix here. "The soup is innocent," I respond with as much of a reassuring smile as I can muster.

"Oh good, because I don't think there's any other food left now that the guys have gone through the line. I'm Sasha by the way."

"Cassidy."

"Is it always like this?" she asks, her wide gray eyes scanning the hall. My eyes narrow in suspicion. How could she not know this by now? Unless she's…

Sasha must sense my distrust, because she takes her bowl off the tray and sets it on the table very carefully. "I live next door. Well, technically I live next door to Mia and Alexei, who do live next door, but that's why this is all so different. I've been going home most nights to feed my dog but tonight I'm working here late so I thought I'd see how the food is." She stirs her plastic spoon idly through the soup.

"And?"

She grins. "I think I'll be hotfooting it home tomorrow night."

"And you work for ACI? Way out here?"

She shakes her curls no. "Only temporarily for this. The rest of the time I'm a graphic designer, but for the last month I've been Mia's assistant fetching and carrying, driving people into town or back from the boat launch. That kind of thing."

Huh. I hadn't thought about how the war games might contribute to the local economy, but I can see that it might if it was handled correctly.

"Is there anything interesting in town? Sorry, that came out wrong but you know what I mean."

She nods with twinkling eyes and finishes chewing before answering. "Probably not. There's the usual ice cream place, used bookstore that never has anything new, and a hardware store. I used to think that was pretty boring too but I'm learning it has mystic significance in town. Don't think that applies to non-residents though. Still, if you like hardware stores, you'll find it right on the main street, one up from the marina."

Yeah, think I'll be skipping that trip into town unless something major comes up. Sasha and I chat a little more as we finish eating. But I'm not at my most social and it's clear she's feeling way out of her depth with the crowd of — I'm not sure what to call them, but you can scent the testosterone in the air.

Even more so when a man I haven't seen before stalks up to our table. "Sasha, what the hell are you doing in here?"

"Eating, Cash. Like everyone else." Sasha casts her eyes demurely down, but even though I've only known her ten minutes, I know that's not who she is. The man is frowning. He's dressed in jeans and a dark gray t-shirt, but everything about him screams military. "You're done, Sasha. If you're still hungry, I'll feed you."

Sasha instinctively licks her lips, and I slap my hand over my mouth to hide my grin. These two need to get a room and hash this out. I'm guessing Cash has the same idea because he's tugging Sasha up by her elbow, then frowning down at her tray and dishes. "Hey, don't worry about those I'll take care of them." I don't know what made me volunteer that, but he flashes me a smile of thanks and I can see what has Sasha all hot and bothered. Sasha rolls her eyes at him, but lets him lead her out of the tent. Briefly she looks back and mouths, 'thank you' at me. I wave and set about collecting both our dirty dishes. I still haven't heard from Burke and now I'm starting to get worried.

Finally, I text him. **Everything OK?**

His response takes a while and I wish I knew if he was debating it or was busy and didn't see my message right away. Anyway, what comes back is **I'm fine. Can you bunk in with the women tonight?**

I shouldn't feel hurt, but I do. And a little queasy. But mostly that's because I don't know what's really going on and I know I'm jumping to conclusions since I don't have enough information to work with. It's still light out, so I still don't respond to Burke. Instead, I head back to my work tent and fire up Betsy. I know I promised to stick to my job but this *could* be an emergency.

I gasp when I finally locate Burke standing in front of a flattened tent. He's on the official radio talking to someone but his body posture is tight and periodically he scans the shore and the woods as if looking for something. Or someone. So maybe this is why he doesn't want me out here tonight. That makes sense, except why not come and tell me? Unless he's planning on staying. I stand up and start pacing the empty walkways between desks. When I check back on Betsy, I can see that a contingent of four more tough guys has arrived by the destroyed tent. So he's not out there by himself. I sit down again, feeling a little unnecessary. I type out a quick reply.

Ok and at the last minute add a sad emoji face.

His response is quicker this time. **Thanks babe.**

Bring Betsy home now.

There's a pause and then, **please?**

I send him a rolling eyes emoji but I bring Betsy back. There's nothing more I can do and that by itself is frustrating. I like taking charge of things. It makes me feel more in control, which always seems completely obvious to me, but everyone else just looks at me funny when I say this. I head out to see if my abandoned cot is still available. My life sucks. Because in case everyone, including Burke, forgot, all my clothes and toiletries were in that tent.

Burke

Thank fuck Cassidy wasn't here when it happened. She might have been killed or kidnapped. Of course I can't tell her that yet. For one, I think she'd insist on camping out here on a matter of principle. And then she'd decide I needed her protection. It's endearing and kinda cute that she wants to protect me, but also mostly pointless. Particularly now that we know we're dealing with real criminals and not just random losers. Although anyone that thought that didn't know the market value of the inflatable that was found on the shore. Not the kind of thing you can pick up at the military surplus store. Not the legal kind, anyway.

Whoever they are, they're gone now. At least for the moment. The tent situation was intended as a diversion while their compatriots picked them up on the beach — some kind of pre-arranged rendezvous, considering we'd confiscated the original boat. Bet that pissed them off.

But we know more than they think because the intention of starting a fire literally fizzled. Thank God, because the grass on the bluff is pretty dry and that could have led to a forest fire. Fucking idiots. I don't know how to break it to Cass, though, that all her clothes were drenched in gasoline. Pretty much a write-off so in between conversations on what I saw, didn't see, and twice as much speculation I'm trying to work out how to get her into town to buy new stuff. It really shouldn't be this hard.

Finally, I just give up on going through channels and walk away. I need to find Cassidy and explain some of this shit. Because I'd bet my last dollar, she's got her cement trowel out and is putting some of the finishing touches on one of those walls she's so good at. Did I say I like smart girls? I do, but they're not easy.

It takes me awhile to track her down, but I finally find her in one of the tents sitting on the edge of a cot and looking forlorn.

"Princess?"

She looks up, startled, and then stands to push

me out. "You can't be in here! No men allowed."

"But I'm your man. And you're here."

She's stands outside the tent clutching her elbows. "You didn't bring my things? Does that mean…"

I sigh. I was hoping to delay this bit, at least until I got a kiss. "Your stuff is ruined, baby. They threw gasoline over everything."

She looks startled. "You mean it wasn't an accident? I thought the tent just collapsed."

"No. No accident. They were trying to start a fire as a diversion. The only real victim was our clothing. Which in the scheme of things is better than the alternative, I guess."

"I guess." She grimaces, rubbing at her side as if it's bothering her.

"You hurt yourself, Cass?"

"Hmmm? Oh no, just feeling a little off. Probably just cramps."

Nothing will get a man to change the conversation faster than talk about a woman's… um, you know, that stuff. I'm no better.

"So I was thinking we could head into town and get some new gear. At least the basics."

She frowns again. "Maybe tomorrow? I'm really not feeling that hot. I think I just want a hot drink and to lie down for a while. I wish we could do that together." She bites her lip like she's worried she confessed too much.

"Okay, well, how about we go to the mess hall and you can rest while I get you food and that drink?"

She nods and leans on me a bit while we walk slowly towards the big dining tent. She must really not be feeling that hot. She's looking a little pale, too. Surreptitiously, I swipe a hand across her forehead. It's a little warm but not burning up.

"Thanks, mom," she rolls her eyes at me and offers a weak smile.

I frown at her in concern. "You don't look very good, Cass. Maybe we should swing by medical first."

"I'll be fine. They'll send me home at the first sign of anything and I don't want to do that. Who would look after Betsy?"

"She's a drone, Cass. Not a dog or a child."

"I know but…" She hunches over, her arm banded around her middle, and throws up into the nearby bush.

That's it. As soon as she seems done with emptying her stomach, I scoop her up as gently as I can and practically run to the first aid tent. The only thing that keeps me to a fast walk is I don't want to jostle her. She's sweating slightly and her gaze is unfocused. Someone opens the tent door for us and I carry her in. There's a sort of rudimentary exam table in the center of the room and I set her down there. In seconds I'm pushed out of the way, although questions come at me from all sides and they take her temperature. Twenty minutes later, a man — I'm guessing he's a doc? — pulls me outside the tent. "The helicopter is on its way. There won't be room for extras.."

"What's wrong with her?" Now I'm seriously worried. I was thinking food poisoning, but she's young and healthy.

"Appendix. Do you know her family? Or I can get someone to look it up on her emergency contact sheet." He raises an inquiring eyebrow and I say, "I'll do it. I haven't met them yet but might as well introduce myself now. Can I go with her?"

"Not enough room. No guests on the medivac. But if you leave now, you can probably get to the hospital about the time she gets out of surgery."

Fuck. Well, there's no question about my priorities, just execution on transportation.

I watch as they load Cass into the red and white helicopter that landed on the airstrip, the one everyone is supposed to be trying to capture. They had to suspend the games early for the day so it could land without being paintballed - I can just imagine trying to explain that one. But nobody seems to mind. I think this will go down in ACI history as the least effective war games ever. But at least it has authenticity to its credit. Whatever can get fucked up has. As soon as the helicopter lifts off, I head off to figure out how to follow Cass to the mainland as fast as possible. But first I have to finagle her contact info out of someone and I know just who will have it.

Missy writes it all down for me on a sticky note without saying a word. I wonder how her conversation with her informants went? But I don't dare ask. I've got more important things to attend to.

I head down to the marina while ringing Cass's parents. If I wasn't so worried about her I'd be shaking in my boots when a big booming voice says, "Hello?"

"Hey, is this the Van Houen residence?"

"Who the hell wants to know?"

"I'm…" oh, what the fuck, "I'm Cassidy's fiance."

"The hell you are. I think I'd know if my daughter was engaged."

"It's very recent. But that's not why I'm calling. She's headed to the hospital."

There's a long silence before her dad's voice turns ominous. "What did you say your name was?"

I don't miss his use of the past tense. Maybe I'd better explain a little faster. "It's her appendix, sir. They think it's ruptured or about to. They've airlifted her to Seattle. I'm on my way there now. And the name is Burke Jamieson."

"Let me talk to her mother. Someone will call you back." And he hangs up abruptly. Guess that went about as well as could be expected.

I was so distracted by the conversation I didn't realize I had already arrived at the marina, but there I stand, with three or four salty-looking fishermen lounging on a bench staring at me. I say three or four because the fourth is ever so slightly more normal looking, so he's the one I walk up to.

"I need to get to Seattle as fast as possible."

He looks over both shoulders slowly. "Am I on one of those TV shows? With the pranks?"

"No." God, how long is this going to take? "My fiancee was just airlifted to the hospital, they wouldn't let me onboard. Who can give me a ride?"

Surprisingly, the oldest and grouchiest of the lot speaks up. "Being in a rush won't get you there any faster, son. Happens my nephew's got a fancy boat he never uses. 'Bout time he took it out. I'll give him a call."

And he does, with the slickest smart phone I've ever seen, although I don't think he's a fan based on the way he's frowning down at the screen and sort of pecking at it with his fat index finger. "Damn phone," he mutters as he holds it up to his ear. Then all he says is "get down here, someone needs a ride in your fancy boat." He hangs up before anyone could possibly have responded to that. Does that mean…?

"Boy will be down here in a few." He nods at me and leans back on the metal railing with peeling paint. I'm sure my expression is skeptical because I'm extremely doubtful. Maybe I should be finding someone else? Because what if this nephew never shows and I've wasted half an hour standing here. And for all I know, the nephew only has a rowboat.

★ ★ ★

Burke

I think twice about that conclusion when a man about my age but with serious swagger saunters down the wide sidewalk that passes as the marina's esplanade. He looks really familiar in a celebrity sort of way. He bears a striking resemblance to rockstar Todd Kipling, but there's not a visible tattoo anywhere so it can't be him. He's got the same tousled hair, but based on the breeze coming off the water I'm guessing that has more to do with nature than styling.

"Uncle Lou? You know you don't pay by the minute anymore? And besides, I pay the phone bill so you could maybe give me a sentence more over the phone before I bust my ass getting down the hill?" The man sounds affectionately exasperated so I not only deduce that the old crusty gentleman is Uncle Lou but that this is pretty much his normal mode of behavior.

The younger man turns to me. "Guessing you're the one needing a ride? What's up? Island life driving you mad?"

"No. My fiancée was medevacked to Seattle. I need to get to her. Your uncle said you have a boat?"

"That I do. Well, sounds to me like a valid reason to shake the cobwebs off old Bianca. Come on." He gestures down the marina towards the slips with the bigger boats. Huh, maybe it's as fancy as his Uncle Lou was claiming. Which might mean a bigger engine and a faster trip to Seattle. One can hope. The man stops in front of what can only be described as a yacht. A very sleek, fairly new yacht. "Who are you?" I blurt out.

"Didn't Uncle Lou tell you? He can be a bit shy. I'm Todd. Todd Kipling."

I gape like a teenage girl. I'm not proud of that, but there it is. Partly because even though I'm used to sports celebrities and a few admirals, I've never stood talking to someone that can pack Madison Square Garden twice in one day. And secondly, because where are all his infamous tattoos?

"Come on. I thought you were in a hurry?" Todd's tone is amused, as if he knows what's running through my mind. I nod decisively and follow him up the narrow ship's ladder. Todd points to a rope. "Just undo that when I give the signal. The rest we can take care of when we clear the marina." He heads into the cabin and I hear the engine roar to life with the soft hum of really well-tuned machinery. Damn. I grab the rope and look back. When Todd raises his hand, I undo the knot holding the boat to the dock and in seconds we're pulling away. I know enough to coil the rope neatly against the bow and then head in to get some answers.

"So if you're that Todd Kipling, where are all the tattoos? And what are you doing on Embrace Island?"

"I should make you sign an NDA for that, but I'll take pity on you. Nobody would believe it anyway." He nods towards the other chair. "Take a seat. I live here now. Partly because of Uncle Lou, who never had any children and refuses to move. Partly because nobody on the island gives a fuck that I'm Todd Kipling, which means I can live a fairly normal life. As for the tattoos, I'm allergic to the ink. But nobody will buy tickets for a band that doesn't have tattoos. Not unless they're doing evangelical Christian or something and even those guys mostly have ink. So it's all temp stuff. Good quality ones last for about two weeks these days so it's not as bad as it sounds. Plus, now you can print your own so I always make sure the same ones go on the same places. Mostly. Almost got caught once, but I convinced the fan that the photo had been reversed in the magazine." He grins like that was a major coup. I'm still shaking my head over catching a ride with a rock star. And I want to tell Cass. That part hurts because I'll bet she's in surgery right now.

I grab my cell and hurriedly type out a message.

Love you. When you see this, if I'm not there I'm on my way. Stay put!

Maybe that will make her laugh. I still haven't heard from her parents but my phone signal is at almost no bars, which isn't too surprising given we're out in open water now.

"Ready to fly?" Todd asks and I nod. I realize I never told him my name but he must be so used to fans thinking he's going to remember them that not asking is habit. He'll ask if he wants to know.

We're speeding now. But the elegant lines of the yacht mean it's cutting through the smooth water of Puget Sound like it's butter so you can barely feel it. There's no bounce at all. Fuck, I could like this boat.

"So what's wrong with your girl?" He finally asks me when he has to ease off the throttle because of boat traffic.

"Appendix."

"Sucks, man."

I nod. It really does.

An hour later and Todd is letting me off at a marina in downtown Seattle. It's not big, and he's not staying so I literally jump off as he idles the boat next to what is the boating equivalent of the ten minute unloading zone. He already turned down my offer to pay for the gas, so I wave my thanks and start maneuvering through the vehicle and pedestrian traffic towards the main emergency hospital on the hill.

When I get there, I'm somewhat relieved to learn that Cass is still in surgery. It's good that I can be there as soon as they put her in a room, but I hope like hell that she didn't hit any complications. Of course they won't tell me anything. As it was, I had to pull the fiance card just to learn as much as I did. So, somewhat at loose ends, I head down to the cafeteria and the gift shop. Maybe I can find something to cheer her up once she's awake.

That's also when I remember to check my phone. Her parents, or rather her mom, left me a voicemail message. She's catching the first flight out and will be here sometime tonight. That's good for Cass, I think? I'll have to ask her how she gets on with her mom.

I eat but I couldn't tell you what it was. It was tolerable, but nothing to write home about. But then it is a hospital and I'm more than a little distracted. The gift shop has more to offer. They must know their audience because there is everything cute and cuddly at twice the price it would be in a regular store. Still, when I spot the perfect thing, I grin and gladly hand over my credit card. It won't make that big a dent.

Then I head back up to the surgery floor and settle in after telling the nurses at the station who I'm waiting for and making sure they know I'm not moving my ass until I can see her. They must hear this a lot because they don't even blink.

About two hours later, there's a hand on my shoulder, and I jerk awake. "Mr. Jamieson?"

"Um, yeah?" I try to get my head back in the game. It's not working so great. "Your fiancée is out of recovery and on her way to her room. Do you want to join her there?" There's only a hint of laughter, and maybe that they'd like the big lump out of their waiting room in her voice. I nod and smile weakly and she gives me a room number while pointing down a hallway.

I wake up more fully as I walk, checking room numbers as I go. When I find 2235 the door is open and I peer inside. The room is pale blue and full of medical equipment. Cass is lying in the hospital bed looking absolutely tiny. But her color is better than the last time I saw her and I breathe out with relief. Her eyes pop open and she smiles wide. "Burke! You came." Her voice is croaky and barely above a whisper, so I hurry over and scoot a chair up to the side of the bed.

"Of course I came, princess. Wasn't going to be any fun without you. How are you feeling?"

"Icky." She pouts, and I can tell that the painkillers are still making her loopy.

"So before you go to sleep, I've got two things for you. Your mom is coming in tonight. She should be here in a few hours and I found you this." I hold up her present from the gift shop. It's a big pink-enameled A that I guess was supposed to be a key chain but the thing is huge. I balance it on the nightstand where she can see it, and her smile is incandescent.

"Love you," she whispers.

I lean down to drop a kiss on her forehead, and her eyes close. She's out of it, which doesn't surprise me.

And while I love hearing those big important words from her lips, I'm not counting my chickens until she says them to me sober. Still, it's a positive sign, and she seems to be resting comfortably, so I lean back in the chair and simply watch her.

Cassidy

Why couldn't my appendix decide to act up closer to home? On top of missing out on the games stuff, now I have to worry about traveling. Although I'm not that sad about missing out on the games. Quite frankly Betsy, Burke, and some of my new friends are what made it interesting. And yes, I probably should put Burke first on the list, but I don't want him getting a swelled head. His ego is plenty healthy as it is.

And now I've got him and my mom fussing over me. Sometimes they collaborate — making me get up and walk down the hall when I'm not in the mood, and sometimes they glare friendly daggers at each other. Mostly over where I'm going when I get out of the hospital later today. Mom wants me back in Ohio at home in my old bedroom. Burke wants me anywhere else because he knows he won't be allowed within sixty feet of my bedroom if I go with Mom. I'm not sure where I want to be, but I'm guessing it will be a week or two before I can do everything without assistance. And regardless, I've no idea how I get there from here because being folded up on an airplane right now does not sound pleasant. Or even like I could manage it without passing out.

Right now my mom is pitching her side with the confident assumption of an army general that I'm not going to question her decisions. "Now Cassy, Dad has already made up your bed with your favorite sheets and he's ready to go to the grocery store. Is there anything in particular you want to eat? I was going to make all of your old favorites."

Wait. She still has my favorite sheets from more than ten years ago?

"Mom..."

"What?" She's busy tapping things on her phone. She's never figured out how to do abbreviations (or she simply refuses to) so she types everything out exactly. And she's a librarian, so she likes really specific long words. I roll my eyes while I wait for her to finish typing.

"Cass?" Mom looks up finally.

"Mom, I'm not going home." Her face falls with disappointment.

"I promise I'll come soon for a long visit and we can do all that cooking together."

"But what…? Where will you go? You can't go home in that condition. And Burke, as nice as he is, I don't trust him to take care of you properly." God help me if Burke ever hears that one. He'll go so overprotective, I'll be wrapped in padding just to walk to the bathroom.

"Mom, I'm thirty. Almost thirty-one. Anything Burke doesn't know how to do, I can tell him." Of course he walks back in my room, right at that moment. I see his lips twitch and a serious twinkle appears in his eyes, promising I'll hear more about this later. But he glances at my mom and wisely keeps his mouth shut.

"But California is so far away." Mom is still not done.

"So is Ohio which is why I'm not going there

either." Now I've got both of them looking at me with shocked expressions. I'm a little scared now to think about Burke sitting down at our family Thanksgiving. He might switch sides in the Big Scrabble Debate that always follows the meal. God help us all if my mom gets reinforcements.

"I found a vacation rental just outside the city that is available for the next two weeks. It's not big, but it looks comfortable. Burke, I was hoping you could stay?" I don't want to take him for granted here. I mean, I really want to, but I know he has a job that he pretty much abandoned to come find me in the hospital. He hasn't said anything more about it, but it's dangerous to make assumptions.

"Princess, I already told you I'm following you, no matter what. That sounds like a really good idea. Then you can see the same doc for your checkup. Anita, how about I promise to call you every morning and night to check in and you can issue any orders for the day?"

"Video call?" she counters. My mom is a master negotiator.

"No problem." Burke gulps slightly, making me think he's a tiny bit worried about that. My mom's eyes sharpen, but she's smiling slightly. I think she's got him right where she wants him, which is sort of funny to watch.

She stands up and drops a kiss on my forehead.

"Then I'm going to go check out of my hotel."

"How are you going to get a flight that fast?" I ask, concerned.

"Oh, I've already got the reservation. I would have pushed it out further if I needed to. I'll be back to say goodbye before they release you, sweetie." And with a cheerful wave she disappears into the hospital corridor. I'm suspicious that she expected this exact outcome all along. I'm still gaping after her when Burke comes round and takes the now empty chair.

"I like your mom but I'm scared of her," he admits ruefully.

"It's the librarian in her. She scares most people."

"On the plus side, she only threatened to castrate me once. That's a good sign, right?"

I ponder this one. "Not sure. She faints at the sight of blood." She does like him, a lot. She finally admitted that to me yesterday, but she's never going to let go of the parental upper hand by letting him know. Still, she was already rearranging the seating chart for Thanksgiving, so he's basically in. And because my dad won't even raise an eyebrow if Burke has Mom's seal of approval, she's the only real barrier to full family membership.

I watch Burke haphazardly pack up my things. Which since I was rushed here, and I lost all my luggage before leaving the island anyway, consists of the hospital 'freebies'. I know those will end up on my insurance bill and then there are the few things he and Mom bought for me. Oh well, I'm alive, and if I lie perfectly still, I feel pretty good.

And there is my dilemma because I'm also horny as hell. All that sexual tension that was building before the tent got attacked, combined with the relief of surviving an emergency. And all I want is to get close to Burke. Really close. But it hurts to laugh, so how we can do any of the things I'm imagining is beyond me. Last night I woke up to find him sitting in the chair, bent over with his face planted on my bed and his long arms draped over my legs protectively. I wanted to drag him into the bed with me and snuggle — okay, I wanted to do a lot more than snuggle but... my physical body is in no shape for that. God, I just need to get well and figure all this out. I don't have the patience to be sick right now.

"You really mean it, about coming back with me to Virginia?"

"Yeah. I do." He looks up from the small bag he's packed with a smile.

"But what about your job?" I don't know why I'm so fixated on that, but maybe because I can't imagine abandoning everything I've worked for. Then again, if there was no other choice, would I drop it all to be with Burke? Honestly, probably not. Not for the first week, and then I'd feel all sad and weepy and run after him. Does that count as a yes? Does it mean I'm not in love with him enough?

"Stop overthinking things, Princess. I told you we have all the time in the world."

"But how can you be so sure? About me, I mean?"

He shrugs. "I just am. And it's okay that you're not built the same way. In fact, I'm really glad you're not exactly like me." He leans down to give me a slow lingering kiss that has me twining my arms round his neck. "In more ways than one, Cass." With a grin, he tugs my arms away and stands up.

"Now, how about you write me a shopping list so I can go get what we need? I have to pick up the rental car too so I'll be gone for a while."

I rattle off everything I can think of. It's not much and for food I leave it to what he's comfortable cooking. I don't know the stores here or what's easy to get to. Anything will be better than hospital food at this point. I haven't even been here that long and already I'm tired of the entire menu.

When he's gone, I lean back against my pillows, angled carefully not to bend me too much in the middle and realize I miss him already.

10

★　★　★

Burke

I've got a bit of a surprise for Cass, and I can't wait to see her face. Instead of the second-floor apartment she thought we were renting, I arranged for something much better.

And because she's crazy, she thought she was paying for it and I think tried for the cheapest thing she could find. But that's definitely not happening. When I rang up the owner to pick up the key and we got to talking, they exchanged the apartment for a lakeside cabin that's all on one level. They're technically not renting it out until later in the season but I think we both walked away happy with the arrangement. And I've been able to get in and make the bed (damn straight we're sleeping together again, finally) and get the groceries stowed away. Now all I need to do is fetch Cass and let her get settled. She's had a helluva week.

Just as I'm locking up to go get her, my phone buzzes with an incoming text from Davis. **Trying to**

reach your gf. Does she know Bob Irskine?

Gf? It takes me a minute - oh, girlfriend. Got it. **Will ask when I get back. What's up?**

Confessed to tent fire. Motive unknown. Jealous lover?

Fuck. The idea of anyone setting out to intentionally hurt Cass makes me see red. And while I didn't get the sense that she had any serious prior relationships — based on all that blushing — we've never really sat down and talked about it. And I really don't want to start interrogating her over something that's not her fault. But I also really want to know what this guy is to her. Double-fuck.

I drive back to the hospital in the only rental that was available that wasn't a tin can. Meaning I'm cruising in a massive SUV that feels like a truck without the style, in a downright funk. I find Cass sitting on the edge of the bed, dressed for the first time since she left the island and looking like she should be back in bed.

"Hey, princess," I say as softly as I can, but my nerves are still wound tight. Cass looks up with a tight smile. "Hey, they told me as soon as my ride got here I could go, but it has to be via a wheelchair to the door. Some kind of regulation. I'll just ring the nurse." She winces as she reaches for the call button so I reach a long arm over and do it for her.

"Cass, while we're waiting, does the name Bob Irksine mean anything to you?"

She frowns hard while her brain churns. "Um, yeah. That's the name of one of the guys that's supposed to report to me. Assuming I can ever get back to my job."

"So not a jealous lover?"

"No." She half laughs and then groans. "Where did you get that idea? And don't make me laugh, I might have to hurt you."

She can, as much as she wants, because the relief that washes over me has me weak in the knees. I quickly text Davis back. But I don't wait for a reply before slipping my phone back in my pocket. He'll sort it out.

"Why were you asking, anyway?" Cass is frowning at me, little tired pain lines showing around her eyes.

"Apparently he's the one that trashed the tent."

"Really? So it wasn't a diversion for the people with the boat?"

"I'm not sure they've ruled that out, but evidently they think he did the tent. Who's your manager? I'll call and make sure Bob is not a factor."

"No, you won't. I can handle it."

"Cassidy."

"Burke." She stares me down in a way that I can

both see her mother in her (good thing I like the woman) and why they're making her a manager. I'm not going to win this round so I change the subject. "I've got a surprise for you, but not until we get out of this place."

She rolls her eyes like she knows I'm avoiding the inevitable capitulation, but we're both interrupted by the arrival of an orderly with a wheelchair.

In no time flat I've got her settled in the SUV, looking like she's ready to collapse after the exertion of it all and we're pulling out of the parking lot. I was going to tell her about the new location but she's already asleep so I figure it'll keep.

She doesn't wake up until I turn off the engine in front of the beach cabin. The beach is attached to a lake, not the ocean, so the house sits right up against the shoreline.

"Hmm? This doesn't look like the picture online." She frowns sleepily at the facade of the small house.

"That's because the owner and I made a switch to this place. No stairs for you to deal with, princess."

"Um. I'm too tired to care right now, but when I wake up properly, you and I are going to have a talk about making executive decisions. But I appreciate the thought." She adds as an afterthought. Now I want to roll my eyes. Life with Cass is never going to be boring.

"Let me help you down and then you can go to sleep thinking of all my bad habits you want to change."

She gets a funny little dent between her eyebrows. "I don't want to change you, Burke. That would be counterproductive."

Of course she doesn't elaborate, so I help her into the bedroom where I'd already made the bed and pulled the covers back. By the time I go back and lock up behind us, she's out like a light. I pull the covers back over her and make sure there's a glass of water on the nightstand before going into the kitchen to make something to eat. I've got about an hour before Cass's mom, Anita, will be expecting our agreed on video call and I need to make sure the place passes inspection. When they say the military prepares you for anything in life, I never thought they meant your future mother-in-law.

Cassidy

When I wake up from my nap I feel so refreshed that I forget why I was in bed in the first place and stretch my arms up over my head. My resulting groan has Burke rushing into the room. "Cass?"

"Sorry, I'm fine. Just pulled on the stitches a bit. Give me a minute." I try to breathe deep and gradually the pain recedes. This time I move gingerly to push myself up. It's light outside, but not nearly as bright as earlier.

"What time is it?"

"About seven. Your mom said not to wake you but she'll talk to you in the morning."

"Was she upset?"

"About?"

"My not going back with her."

Burke shrugs. "Not noticeably. She made me give her a virtual tour of the place, peeked in on you. Told me to be sure to feed you lots of leafy greens to keep you regular."

"Oh God," I groan into the pillow I plunk over my face.

He chuckles. "Nothing wrong with being regular, babe."

I just shake my head under the pillow. "I am not six!"

"No, you're not. And I cannot goddamn wait until we can pick up where we left off. So if leafy greens are what will get you there fastest then expect to get really tired of spinach." He's practically growling, and I lift the pillow in amazement. His eyes are focused on my panties, just below the hem of my t-shirt.

"Um, about that…" I push myself up to standing and

he rushes over to my side. Sweet, but unnecessary.

"I'm starving, Burke. But after we eat, can we talk about maybe… um…" I blush as I make myself meet his eyes. They soften from closed off need to understanding as my half sentence soaks in.

"Sweetness, you're in no shape to fuck."

"I know." I grimace. Trust me, I know. "But maybe if… I don't know, but first I need food."

"Right. Are you sure you don't need help?" He's reaching for me as I shuffle towards the small attached bathroom.

"Not six!" I shout as I shut the bathroom door behind me.

When I come out again, he's disappeared into what I think is the kitchen. There's some banging going on and a few muttered swearwords so I proceed in that direction with caution.

"Safe in here?" I ask from the doorway after a long pause to admire his ass. If he's going to bend over like that… I'm going to objectify him without apology, now that I know he isn't ever going to report to me at work.

Burke stands up and sort of sweeps me onto a chair then drops a kiss on my lips. I wish he'd linger there, but he's already back to flipping things on the stove.

"Whatcha making?" I ask curiously.

"Pancakes." He frowns as he flips the little golden circles. "I only know how to make three things and this is the fastest."

"Is there syrup?"

"Yeah. The real deal, coming up."

He pulls a fully laden plate out of the oven and takes it over to the small table in front of the window overlooking the lake. I slide off the bar stool and head over with more energy in my step. Pancakes for dinner? I'm in. I really am starving so once I've got a stack dripping with maple syrup I dig in and don't look up until I've taken the edge off. When I finally do, it's to find Burke watching me with a bemused expression on his face.

"What? Did you think I was going to turn this down and ask for a salad?"

He shakes his head. "No… I just didn't think you were *that* hungry."

I sigh, licking a bead of syrup off my lower lip. "I was. I might still be." I bite with enthusiasm into one of the bacon strips he cooked. I've probably eaten enough for now, but it tasted so good. I nibble on bacon as Burke goes back to his own dinner and polishes it off. Now, how do I convince him I really need sex to wrap up the healing process?

I try the direct approach. "Burke, I really, really need sex right now."

He chokes, "Wow, I feel so objectified."

"No, you don't," I grumble at him good naturedly.

He grins. "Okay, lucky and frustrated. Babe, your mom would castrate me if you tore open your incision. Plus, I'm really not turned on at the idea of making you hurt."

"Isn't there something..." I'm on the edge of whining here, it can't be pretty.

He sucks syrup off the end of his finger, and as my eyes follow his lips, my pussy floods with need. I shift uncomfortably.

Burke eyes me thoughtfully. "Maybe. But it's going to have to be more like phone sex. In person."

I'm confused, but I let him help me up and follow him down the short hall to the bedroom. "You get ready for bed, Cass."

"Can I be naked?"

He heaves a long-suffering sigh, but his eyes are twinkling. "I guess."

I strip carefully. I've already learned the lesson about making sudden moves. Then I brush my teeth.

Burke is already on the bed when I return, leaning against the headboard, his worn jeans unbuttoned but otherwise still clothed. He pulls back the covers next to him. "In you get, princess."

I roll my eyes at the term, wishing I had the health and nerve to do more than simply walk from point a to point b. I crawl under the covers and wonder where this is going as Burke tucks the blanket in around me.

"You ready?" He sounds hesitant and I look up at him, questioning.

He smiles slightly. "Can't say as I've ever done this before, Cass."

"If it really makes you uncomfortable…" I trail off. I don't want to coerce the guy.

"I'm not uncomfortable *yet*, princess. But I've got a feeling I'm about to be." He clears his throat.

"Alright, I want you to close your eyes and imagine you're on a beautiful tropical beach."

I dutifully close my eyes, suspicious that he's just trying to lure me to sleep.

"You're walking along the water's edge, completely naked. The sun is teasing the curve of your ass, the top of your tits, making you hyper aware of your skin. You feel your nipples harden and a light breeze teases them into hard buttons. You reach up and take the weight of your tits in your hands, rubbing gently against your nipples trying to sooth the ache."

Without realizing it, I've done exactly as he said,

my fingers lightly moving over my breasts, the bedclothes pushed down around my waist.

Burke's voice sounds a little uneven when he continues, "Your pussy is feeling wet and achy. But if you let go of your breasts, they'll ache too. You wish frantically for your lover. You think about what it would be like if he were there with you, on the sand. His thick cock hard and ready for you."

There's a long pause and I peek up at Burke to find him swallowing hard. I glance down. His jeans are tight, right at my eye level, and I see him shift uncomfortably. I reach a hand over and tug lightly to free his cock.

"Cass..." Burke rasps.

"What? I haven't moved an inch. Keep talking. I think my lover was approaching," I encourage him while licking my lips at the magnificence before me. If I turn my head just a little and hold him just so... I take the bulbous head of his cock into my mouth and swirl my tongue. This is what I needed. Well, I need more too. But I needed him inside me somewhere, to suck him into me. Just this small amount of contact sends fire down my nerve endings, straight to my core.

"Um. Right. Your lover pushes you to your knees in the warm sand and then his hand connects with your ass, slapping your bare skin, punishment for starting without him."

The vision fills my brain, and I suck long and hard on Burke's throbbing cock. Needing to feel that sense of domination he's describing.

"Like that, did you? Oh fuck, Cass. Shit, I'm close."

Encouraged, I lave my tongue into the slight grove it found, and I feel his leg beneath me quiver. I do it again. "Cassy!" he shouts, as he spills his seed down my throat. I push his cock deep into my mouth as it continues to pulse. Instead of triggering my gag reflex, which I fully expected, it's like his girth sooths the emptiness allowing my body to relax. Well, parts of it anyway. I can feel my pussy clasping at air, eager for more.

Burke gasps for breath as I slowly lick him clean. I keep my hand loosely wrapped around his cock because it feels nice, and I want to be as close as my body will allow. "Right, your lover takes you to task for making him cum before you. He enjoyed it, but he's not pleased with you. He's going to make you cum three times now to make up for it." His tone is wry, and he gently pries my hand away from his cock. Oops, guess I was squeezing when he mentioned making me cum three times.

He keeps his hand laced with mine, his thick fingers spreading mine apart, pressing into the sensitive skin at their base. I shift my legs restlessly.

"Where were we? Oh yes, you're on your hands and knees in the sand. Now that your ass is a beautiful shade of pink and tingling from your punishment, he spreads those cheeks until you can feel the ocean breeze on your hot pussy. So wet and glistening in the sun. The wind teases you, making that little clit throb, but your lover isn't going to let the wind pleasure you before him. He pushes his cock into you in one long stroke. He's big and you feel every inch as he takes you, claims you without mercy. You can't move. All you can do is stay where you are, your thighs straining as he pounds into you, slick with your juices, faster and faster until you can no longer tell if his huge cock is coming or going. You just have to wait as you feel the energy build. Until finally, finally your body can't take it anymore and it lets go. Your pussy clenching around him, forcing him to still until he too can do nothing more than fill you with his cum, sending it deep until it overflows and drips down your thighs."

Oh dear God. Without even moving a muscle, my body responds to his voice and I'm cumming so hard I see stars. I bring our joined hands down and bite into the side of his hand. Not too hard but I need, I want…

Slowly I open my eyes to see Burke smirking at me. "Was it good for you?"

I nod dazedly. "I just have one question."

"Shoot."

"Where the hell did you learn to talk like that?"

Burke

Cass looks the most relaxed I've seen her since they lifted her into that air ambulance. Her amber eyes are sated but also fired with curiosity. Staring into them, I suddenly feel this rush of fierce love wash over me. I'm no longer depressed about the next phase of my life, I can hardly wait to get started. As long as Cass is there next to me. I knew I was in love with her before, but now she's somehow sunk roots deep within me. I can't imagine my life without her in it. I don't even have the words to express to her how I'm feeling right now, so instead I clear my throat. "There's a lot of sitting around and waiting at swim meets. One day when I was about fifteen I got bored and fished this paperback out of my mother's bag. I don't remember what it was called, but it didn't take me long to find the steamy scenes. They were along the same lines."

"Wow. Did you and your mom start a book club?" Cass is openly laughing at me. I remember how hard it was to look my mom in the eye after reading that book. Okay, parts of it. I didn't worry too much about reading the bits in between the sex.

"God, no." I groan, just thinking about it. "I don't think she ever even knew I read it. Fucking embarrassing knowing your mom is reading that shit."

"Hey!"

I grin down at her outrage. I'm not sure if it's on behalf of steamy romance readers in general, or my mom, or this book in particular. "Relax, princess. I sure like where it took us tonight. Now I have a question for you. Where did you learn to suck a cock like that?"

I'm honestly not sure I want to know the answer. And even less so when she blushes a deep fiery red.

"Did I do it wrong?"

"Hell no. If you weren't in recovery, I'd lie down and beg you to do it again," I confess.

Cass smiles shyly. "Really?"

I nod.

"That was the first one I ever gave. I went on instinct."

I stare down at her pretty face, shocked. "I think we just found your super power. You'd better reserve it for your faithful sidekick from here on out."

Her eyes brighten. "I'd like that." She sighs lightly and her eyelids drift close. I watch her for a few more minutes as her breathing deepens and slows into a gentle, steady rhythm.

We haven't talked about her job or the implications that her soon-to-be direct report might have tried to kill her. Makes me wonder if the other men are cut from the same cloth. If I have to, I'll make a few calls but I'm hopeful somebody is going to come to their senses and call the whole thing off. Not that Cass isn't fully capable of the job, but her physical safety shouldn't even be in question. And even if it means she gets seriously mad at me, I'm going to make sure she's safe.

I know she's worried about my job. I figure it's over and it's only a matter of time before I get a call. I'm good with that. My real calling now is Cass and convincing her that I'm definitely sticking around. Once we've achieved that milestone I want to get started on kids. If I can live that long. Seeing her lips wrapped around my cock, knowing she has to be hurting just about did me in. In more ways than one, because the woman has talents. If she can give that kind of blowjob, I may not survive actually sinking my cock into her pussy. I'll die happy, but I'd rather live to do it over and over again.

Watching her sleep, I'm already looking forward to waking up next to her. In a real bed this time, not those damn narrow cots. And eventually she's going to feel well again and that… that's going to make every day a red-letter day. Particularly if she likes morning sex. I sigh. It would be too juvenile to wake her up and ask her. But I really want to.

Cassidy

The next few days pass quickly. I'm sleeping more than I like, but I know it's what I need, so I don't grumble (too much). Burke has now cycled through his entire cooking repertoire and is starting to repeat. Luckily I like what he cooks, but I could see how another week of pizza for breakfast could get old.

I still have niggling doubts about the wisdom of us having a relationship. There's no question the chemistry is there, but am I just a challenge to him? The first woman who didn't trail after him with her tongue hanging out? I'm just not sure and there isn't too much time before one or both of us sacrifices so much that if things don't work out someone is going to get seriously hurt. I'm fretting about this while trying to read a book on my phone about leadership when Burke gets up from the armchair opposite my couch on the porch. He walks around to the other side of the house with his phone pressed to his ear.

See? Another thing we're not completely open with each other about. And that's hardly weird with two people that haven't known each other for more than a couple of weeks. As long as it's not a girlfriend on the phone. I don't really think that. Burke isn't underhanded, he's just idealistic. I try to go back to my book but it's dull as dirt.

Burke comes back. His lips pursed thoughtfully and his eyes are… determined, is the word I'd use. "Who was that?" I inquire as casually as I can manage. I do not want to become one of those insecure girlfriends that has to know where her man is every second of the day.

"More a matter of what than who," he answers, idly bending down to drop a kiss on my lips. "I'm now a free man, princess."

I frown up at him. Did I miss something critical? Was he on parole? Getting a divorce?

He grins down at me. "If you could see your face, Cass. That was ACI, wondering when I'm planning to come back to work. I told them I wasn't. They wanted to know where to send my final paycheck. I said I'd let them know after I talked to you."

"Burke, should you have done that? I know you said you'd follow me but… quitting is so um, final."

"Cassy, my job was over, anyway. Believe it or not, I'm too old for it. They'd have put me in a desk job or I could have left and moved into coaching. Neither really appeals to me. And those options remain options just about anywhere in the world. So you're not going to get rid of me that easily."

"I'm just worried that you'll regret giving up things for me. I'm not that easy to live with."

He sits down on the floor, his back against the couch. His hair has gotten longer just in the last few weeks and it's starting to curl slightly.

Burke turns his head to look at me. "Tell me more."

"I'm obsessively neat," I confess. "I don't like things left out on countertops. My roommates used to get mad at me for putting their stuff in drawers. So I gave up on roommates as soon as I could afford to."

"You can clean up after me anytime, sweetness." He grins and I tug on those curls of his because I can't resist any longer.

"And I sing in the shower. Loudly. Off key and I don't care."

"You're not putting me off, Cass. That sounds adorable."

I roll my eyes. He hasn't heard me. Even I know I screech. I just think everyone deserves to make noise somewhere. I'm working up to the big one, though. "And I'm a blanket stealer. My one boyfriend in college broke up with me because he said I was selfish when I was asleep and it was clearly a sign of my true character."

I peek at Burke to see how he's taking this, but he's just staring at me. "Cassidy. I thought I made it clear. I'm your blanket. You'd better be selfish as hell with me, because I'm going to be that way with you. I want you to be warm and comfortable. You come first. Any prick who thinks otherwise doesn't deserve the time of day from you."

"And that's another thing." I'm getting on a roll now.

"What?" He sighs like he's tired of this game. Except it isn't a game, these things are very real to me.

"When you talk like that, that you'll give me anything I want, or I come first… it's nice in theory, but I feel like I'm taking advantage of you. That I'll start taking you for granted and you'll just let me."

He's openly laughing now, his head thrown back on my midriff. "You really took that superhero thing to heart, didn't you? Princess, I'm a grown man with ten plus years of military experience. Nobody takes advantage of me. Unless I want them to." He reaches for my hand and presses a kiss to my palm. "Cass, you don't have to do absolutely everything by yourself just to prove you can. Let me in, baby."

I stare at him for a long moment. "I'll try," I concede.

"Can't ask for more than that." His eyes crinkle at the corners.

"So I have a confession to make," I say hesitantly.

Burke's eyebrows shoot up. "You robbed a bank while I was making the bed?"

"No, you idiot. I checked my work email while you were making the bed."

"Cass, no working until the doc says you can."

"It wasn't work. It was just email." I frown at him. "Now stop interrupting. I'm glad I did because there's a problem."

Burke just waits for me to finish. I sigh again. "My new job no longer exists. Between my being out sick and the whole tent on fire thing which requires an internal investigation, they're putting that position on hold… indefinitely. So I can either go back to my old job or they offered me a somewhat similar position on the other side of the country. In Sala Bay."

"That's not too far from here, right?"

I nod. "About an hour and a bit."

"And how do you feel about your old job?"

I shrug. "It was okay. But there's nothing new with it, nothing to look forward to or new challenges, so I'm a bit bored."

"Alright, so what about Sala Bay, what's your opinion on that?"

"It's all change, new job, new location, new building, new weather."

"Do you like living in Virginia?"

My shoulders lift halfheartedly again. "It's fine. I don't have any close friends or family there but I've gotten used to it."

"Do you want to go back there and find something else?"

I think about that and what's really bothering me about moving here. Ironic that I'm laid up so close to my potential new home. "Not really. I'm not attached to anything there. It's just familiar."

"Would you rather run off and start a wilderness resort in Alaska?"

"Where did that come from?" I laugh at him, wondering if that's his secret dream.

"Just throwing something out there for contrast. I'll take that as a no."

"Is that something you think about doing someday?"

"Hell no, the water there is colder than it is here. I'm an easygoing guy, princess. Although it's a relatively new dream, what I want right now is a family — a couple of rug rats running around getting into trouble and deciding what superheros they're going to be. While I mow the lawn in obsessively neat stripes so I can look down on my neighbors with superiority."

"You are such a goofball." I'm caught up in his vision of mini Burkes flailing about the backyard, playing pirates. An unfamiliar yearning to be in the center of all that chaos sweeps over me.

"So you're fine with Sala Bay? If I take that job?"

He nods, seemingly unconcerned with where he lives. I can't imagine being that laid back about something so important, but then I've never experienced being transferred all over the world either. Maybe it changes your perspective.

"You said you'd do whatever I want, right?"

"Not exactly." He narrows his eyes at me. "Why? What suddenly popped into that pretty head of yours?"

"I want major decision sex. It's like make up sex only without the fight."

"Did you just invent that?"

"Yes," I confess. "But I still want it."

"Babe, this is where I prove that I won't let you take advantage of me when it's going to hurt you. No sex until the doc says it's okay."

I study his face. He's serious for once and there's no give in his expression. He won't do it. Not until I get the damn doctor's permission. Fine.

I pick up my phone from the cushion it was lying on and dial.

12

★ ★ ★

Burke

Cass is pouting like a real princess. Or at least the spoiled kind that get featured on the gossip rags in the grocery store checkout lane. The doctor, once she finally got a call back, wasted no time letting her know that actual sex was off the table for at least another two weeks. The only thing that keeps me from rubbing her face in it (nicely) is that for once I'd have been grateful to be wrong. But I wasn't.

To distract her, I suggest a drive out to Sala Bay so she can check out the neighborhoods and Cass is on board with that. She's moving around much better now, but we'll keep this to a vehicle tour only. And I stick an extra pillow and blanket in the back just in case she needs to stretch out before we're back here.

It's an interesting drive and I think we both perk up a bit when the big city fades in the distance and the charm of smaller towns starts to emerge. Sala Bay is close enough to the city to enjoy some of the amenities but not so close that it's become a bedroom community. Not yet, anyway.

The ACI building stands out. Easily one of the three tallest buildings in the town, it's nothing special but well kept up. I turn into one of the residential communities so Cass can window shop for houses.

"Ooh, that one's cute!" She points to a small bungalow with a pretty garden. We follow the street out of town to a less dense neighborhood filled with trees and larger houses set back from the road. There are peeks of water in between that suggest we're on a small bluff overlooking the bay.

"Are we in some kind of cult neighborhood or something?" Cass asks with curiosity.

"I didn't see any signs. Although I suppose cults don't advertise much. Why?"

"Because the last three houses we passed had couples working in the front yard and the men were clearly ex-military and the women were bossing them around."

"So you're saying you'd like to live here, then?" I'm teasing, but that does sound like an ACI kind of profile. The single men don't talk about it much but ACI is known for on the job romances and when those guys fall, they fall hard and stay there. If anything, they sink deeper once the kids start coming.

"I don't seem to have the knack of bossing you

yet." She's pouting again.

"Oh, you do just fine, princess. Ready to head back? I've got a surprise for you."

"Really? What is it?"

I shake my head. Christmas is going to be a nightmare in our house. I can see it now.

Cass is looking a little tired by the time I park our rental car in front of the cottage. But she deserves a bit of a treat after a day like today.

"Why don't you go get ready for bed?" I prompt her once we're inside.

"What about my surprise?"

"It's coming."

She gives me a suspicious look but heads down the hallway. I dig around in the kitchen cupboards, acquiring my supplies. It's an odd assortment of ingredients and hardware I haul down the corridor but innovation is just one of my many skills in the bedroom.

"What on earth are you doing?" Cass sounds bewildered, more than skeptical as I lay everything out on the nightstand.

"Let the master work," I instruct her. "Lie down."

"Is this going to be messy?"

"Very," I tell her with satisfaction.

"Am I going to cum?"

"Guaranteed."

"Even though the doctor said... and you wouldn't...?"

"Your doctor said no penetration. And that's all you're getting out of me, princess. On the bed, unless you'd rather just go to sleep?"

"I'm going. I'm going." She dutifully lies down on the sheets, her eyes bright with anticipation. Too bad I'm about to cover them with a dishtowel. I fold it over diagonally until it's a narrow strip. Unfortunately, it says *Kitchen* on it but nobody but me is going to be looking at it. I tie it loosely behind her head, but Cass is back to pouting. "How come I don't get to look?"

"Because the mystery will heighten your sensation. I've got a limited scope to work with here, babe."

She settles back, clearly waiting for the show to begin, and I can't help but grin. Shy Cass is gone for good, it seems. I drape the second dish towel over her surgery incision. No point in complicating things by getting stuff where it shouldn't be. Then I get started with the main event.

One egg white, beaten with a tiny bit of sugar to make it less gloppy and a paintbrush some kid left behind, and I set to work on my masterpiece. I tease her dainty nipples with the brush until they're standing at attention, her areolas puckered up into perfect rosettes. Then I dip the paintbrush in the egg white and set about tracing it over her delicate skin, connecting freckles, writing out my name, whatever suits my fancy. Periodically Cass giggles or makes a smart remark, but that's only because the intended effect hasn't set in yet. I blow gently over my artwork to get the process started as I watch her squirm slightly.

"No touching, Cass. If you move your hands, I'll have to tie them." I warn her and my cock surges at her sudden hiss of an inhale. Too bad because he's not getting any action except my hand tonight. As the egg white dries, it tightens on her skin and I can see that she's starting to feel the tingle. "Hold still, Cass."

I spread her legs slightly with my hands, holding her thighs gently but firmly enough not to let her close them again. Her pretty little pussy is wet and glistening. She wasn't kidding about needing some relief. I trail kisses up her thigh, hinting at my ultimate destination but not delivering. Not yet.

"Burke!" Cass arches her back, her fingers digging into the mattress.

"Patience, princess." I pause to take her nipple into my mouth. Sucking it, then flicking it hard with my tongue. She tries to use her legs to draw me down, but that's not happening. "Do you want me to tie you to the bed?" I ask her.

"Umm, no?" Her hesitancy makes me smile. I have a feeling we'll get there eventually if not tonight. Never been a particular kink of mine, but having Cass spread out before me, for me alone to feast on, is pure decadence and I think I'm getting addicted.

"Then keep those arms and legs flat on the bed, please." After a few seconds, she relents and straightens her limbs. I go back to give her other breast the same treatment, this time nipping the upper curve with my teeth, just enough to make her belly quiver in response. Her body is flushed now, her lips parted.

I return my attention to her pussy, pushing her legs a little bit wider. "So wet, princess. You need to cum, don't you?"

"Yesss," she sighs.

I lave the juncture of her thigh and pussy until she's twisting on the bed. Then I lick her honey until she's gushing out more. Finally, I suck gently on her clit, rolling it on my tongue until I hear her sputter with a keening cry. Then I suck harder, letting the edge of my teeth just scrape against her swollen fresh. She shatters in my arms and I hold her gently so she won't twist her incision. Then I go back to licking her release, unwilling to let any of it go to waste.

When I finally take the tea towel from her face, her gaze is unfocused and heavy-lidded. I gently wash her skin, removing the dried egg, and she sighs, "You're a dangerous man in the kitchen, Burke. I hope your mother doesn't know what you can do with an egg."

I snort, trying not to imagine my mother's reaction because really, nobody needs their parents in their head at a time like this.

Cassidy

I'm bored. And I feel guilty because Burke's done so much for me that I don't want to add keeping me entertained to his list of household chores, which just keeps getting longer, anyway. And I'm ever so slightly irritated with him because he won't sit down and discuss his future career plans. All I get is, "Let's get you settled in your new job, princess. Then I'll figure something out." Gah. I can't remember a time in my life when I didn't have a five-year plan. Even in grade school I had a path charted through to get as many advance placement courses out of the way in high school so I could finish college in three years. It didn't seem strange. This was the sort of stuff my family talked about over the dinner table. That, and Ashley's latest crush, which changed pretty much daily.

So Burke's take each day as it comes attitude is shocking to me. But it suits him and I'm learning to adjust my expectations. Trying anyway. He's been patient with me and at night when I lie here with his arm wrapped around me, I feel so safe and warm.

I eye my phone. I've read all my new ebooks, surfed the web for celebrity gossip. Read all of Burke's old swimming articles, which didn't say much more than he was fast with a promising future. That's when it hits me that I still have Betsy's secondary control app on there. And the games are still going on, through tomorrow I think, unless something else dire has happened.

With excitement, I grab my phone and bring up the app. Mentally crossing my fingers that nobody's put Betsy in a box and the connection will still work. It does. I blow out a breath strong enough to flip my hair up and settle in against my pillows to see what I've missed.

It doesn't look like anybody even bothered to move Betsy. Her camera picks up the same desk and environment as where I left her. Nobody is there. I look at the clock, just about dinner time. I zip her out of the tent and gain some elevation, just in case. I wonder who's winning the games? I'm about to head out to the other airstrip to see if I can tell when I catch a brief glimpse of a couple in a tight lip lock. Oooh, more romance! Wait, it's Violet, her feet dangling as this massive man pins her against a tree. I go in closer just to make sure she's in agreement with this situation. It doesn't take long to tell that she definitely is. And… it's that same guy that was glowering at her so intensely that one day. The man she said totally 'floated her boat'. I give her a mental high five and give them their privacy. Well, at least from me. They're kind of going at it in a completely public place.

My new view point shows Sasha headed through the trees. Her shoulders are slumped and her head is down. I want to hug her tight, just seeing her body language. Where is her hunky soldier? I follow behind her for a bit, wondering where she's going, and I see her take a slightly worn path towards an older house on the shore. That must be her place. Suddenly she picks up speed and starts running. That's when I see that soldier guy was waiting for her on the porch. He stands as she approaches and then swings her wide, his lips fastened on hers. Ah — happy endings everywhere you look. Except… what's that?

There's some kind of slow-moving vehicle driving down the road. It's going well below ten miles an hour and um, there's no driver? How is that even possible? I fly Betsy in for a closer look. Nope, definitely nobody in the vehicle but windows are down and the back is packed tight. And there are wires. Oh my God. It's a car bomb. And not the confetti kind.

"Burke!" I shout, but it doesn't come out very loud because panic is freezing my vocal cords. Thank fuck he hears me anyway and rushes in. He calms a little when he sees me sitting in one piece.

"Princess? What's the matter?"

"Betsy… car bomb… a real one!"

He takes the phone from me, glances at it. "Fuck."

He reaches for the old-fashioned phone on the nightstand and dials a long series of numbers.

"Which wire, Burke? Which wire will stop it?" I'm practically crying with fear for all the people at the other end of that road.

"I don't know sweetness. Pick one." He's distracted so I go back to studying the setup. I know nothing whatsoever about bombs. And there are a lot of wires. On the other hand, if it goes off now, nobody will be hurt. I think. The longer I wait, the less likely that will be the outcome. I set Betsy to work. The first two wires don't do anything. The third though… that one when Betsy tugs on it with everything she's got, there's an odd pop and then I see a flurry of dark movement and sound. Then nothing. The screen is blank, no response.

"Betsy!" I scream down at my phone. Burke is talking to someone urgently, but he sits down on the bed and gathers me close. Tears are running down my cheeks.

He hangs up after about twenty minutes and kisses my temple.

"She gave her life so others could live," I sob into his chest. To his credit, he doesn't laugh. At least not so I can hear him. He just holds me close and rubs my back.

"You did good, Cass. Nobody was hurt, and they were able to put out the small fire with minimal effort."

"Who would do such a thing? That's nothing to do with the war games." I don't know how I know that, but I do.

"No. They finally traced that boat to a new high-powered international crime ring. All the three letter agencies are moving in tomorrow to start an investigation. They've asked ACI to leave all the tents in place so they can hit the ground faster."

"But why bomb people if their cover is blown?"

"Maybe they don't know it is? Or they're just really pissed?"

I gape at him. Thinking about him alone on the shore with that kind of bad guy floating around. I hug him tight, even though my side is aching. "You're never going anywhere without me again." I tell him fiercely.

Burke grins down at me with a slight smirk. "Got you right where I want you, princess."

13

★ ★ ★

Cassidy

Now that the big moment is here, I'm almost afraid to actually see it through. There is such a thing as too much anticipation. I stare down at the ring on my left hand. I'm still not sure how it got there. I mean, I was present, but it wasn't like Burke actually asked me to marry him. He just sort of… charmed me.

I tried to convince him that maybe we should wait until we'd actually had sex, just in case he hated it. He had the nerve to laugh. Hard. I swatted him in annoyance. And then there the ring was. It's gorgeous and not a bit of 'look how big my diamond is' at all. In fact, there is no diamond which suits me down to the ground. Instead, it's a wreath of carved gold leaves, each one curled protectively around a small fiery opal.

I pull up to the garage of our new house and wait for the automatic opener to engage and raise the door. Burke's jeep is already inside but there's plenty of room to slide my new small SUV in next to it.

All this in only two weeks since I accepted the transfer to Sala Bay. In fact, Burke and I never left. We just bought a house, or rather Burke did, but he insisted my name go on the deed too, and we bought all new stuff. Eventually I'll get back to Virginia and box up my things, but probably not for at least another month.

And I love this house. It's just the right size, and the master bedroom gets beautiful morning sun. I know eventually the infamous gray clouds will come back into the sky when summer draws to a close, but for now, it's bright and cheerful.

It still bothers me that Burke gave up his job for me. I know he says he'd have had to make a change anyway, but who knows how I may have limited his options. He does seem sincere when he says he doesn't care and it has been awesome letting him do all the unboxing and putting things away. Even if I have to move them to a better location later.

But not now. Right this minute, I'm not concerned in the least about whether the water glasses are to the left or the right of the sink. All I care about is getting my man naked. Because yes, finally the doctor said I could have sex. What kind of world do we live in where we have to get permission to do the most basic of human activities? The most embarrassing part is I had to get him to write it out on a prescription pad because Burke won't believe me otherwise. To be fair, I did sneak out to my appointment over lunch so he didn't even know I was going. My new doctor's office is only a block away from the ACI building, so that just seemed easier.

Enough about that. I finally find Burke in the back guest bedroom, folding towels. It's like one of those super sexy laundry detergent commercials and I do let my eyes drink him in for a minute. He glances up and smiles warmly. "Hey, princess. When did you get home? I didn't hear a thing."

"Just now. But guess what?"

"You want to move back to Virginia and you don't want to tell me to start boxing everything up?"

I roll my eyes at that one. "Would it be crass of me to say I really want you naked now?"

"You went to the doctor, didn't you?" His smile turns into a slight smirk, like he naturally accepts being the subject of every woman's sexual fantasies.

I nod enthusiastically, practically bouncing with excitement.

Burke pulls me tight against him. "I feel so used," he murmurs as he bites gently on the curve of my neck.

"Ass. I could always go find someone else."

"Like hell you will." He growls playfully into my neck as he swings me up. "Kid gloves are coming off, princess."

I shiver with delight as he carries me into the bedroom.

"How do you want this, Cass? Fast and hard, slow and soft, what?"

"Slow and hard. I want to feel all of you, every sensation. I don't want you to hold back, Burke."

"No danger there." He settles me down on the bed like he's still afraid I might get hurt, and he bats my hands away when I start to unbutton my blouse. "My turn to play, princess."

He takes his time. When I'm finally naked, I'm ready to jump him and plunge down on his cock, which looks like it wants the same thing from the way it's jutting forward. I lick my lips and reach my hand out, but Burke shakes his head. "I won't last two seconds if you touch me now, Cass. In fact, if you want this deep and long, why don't you get on your knees, let me take you from behind."

I think about it. I want to watch his face, but... being able to feel his hands on me while stuffed full of his now erect cock sounds too delicious to pass up. I move to the center of the bed on my hands and knees. And wait.

Then I turn my head to see what's taking so long and there's Burke standing with his legs spread, his eyes fixated on my ass. I lick my lips and feel my clit throb as wetness drips down my inner thighs. "Please, Burke?"

His smile is tight. "Princess, I promise the second time will be better."

I laugh. "What on earth do you mean?"

"I can't make this last. You're too delectable. I'll come back for you. I promise."

I'm still trying to puzzle that out when his cock slides into my core. Firmly, decisively, and oh so slowly.

My mouth is hanging open by the time he bottoms out. I'm so wet there's no resistance but I've never in my life felt so full. So complete. Admittedly, I could count my previous partners on one hand and have fingers to spare, but this is something on a whole other plane of existence.

Burke's hands cover my breasts, holding their weight and torturing them with friction as he rubs my nipples to hard points. His cock is pushing back in, going even deeper, and I nestle back, wanting all of him. He reaches one hand down rather desperately and strums my clit. With one more firm stroke of his cock, he cums deep inside of me. I'm biting my lip as my own release washes over me even as he continues to empty long ropes of cum into my aching pussy. I want more. Already I want him again.

Burke is pressed against my back, his cock still stretching me wide when he gasps, "Give me five minutes."

I wiggle my ass a little and he groans with a laugh. "Fine, two minutes. But don't blame me if you walk down the aisle pregnant."

I turn my head as far as it will go to stare back at him. "Who do you want me to blame? We don't even have a milkman."

He laughs, and I feel the firm grip of his hands on my hips as he slowly pulls out and then flips me over.

"I love you, Cassidy. And your smart mouth." He must because he claims it with his and I can't get another word out for at least ten minutes.

Burke

I never had any doubt that when I finally got to claim Cassidy with my cock, that it would be the best sex of my life to date. Second best was eating her out. Other than being so damn out of control I was like a horny teenager, nothing about that moment was a disappointment. That we had to wait so long only made it that much more intense.

Now I just have to convince her to get married soon before I knock her up because that's coming sooner rather than later. Her mother already thinks we take too damn long to answer the phone when she calls. I don't need to give her more ammunition.

Although she might be a tiny bit on my side when it comes to grandchildren but I don't dare mention that to Cass.

And I'm working on some home-based business ideas because I can't have Cass wearing herself out with her need for neatness. I figure if I'm in the house to keep the basics taken care of I can herd her into the bedroom when she gets home from work. And then convince her with a few back-to-back orgasms not to care if there are a few dishes still in the sink. Because I don't think I'm ever going to get tired of seeing her eyes widen with surprise when she cums. My girl deserves to feel that good every damn day of her life. And it sure as hell is more important than a couple of dirty dishes.

Those guys out there bragging about playing the field? They haven't got a clue about what they're missing. Knowing that I get to wake up to Cass every morning, sink into her warm depths every night, (and maybe in the morning too) has me hard every time I think about it. She's fucking it for me. In every possible way.

And even though I wouldn't wish the scare and pain of surgery on her for the world, I'm fucking grateful it got her off that island. The more I hear about what went down after we left, the less I like it. No way in hell she's going to another one of those things. I have a two-prong strategy to ensure that. One is to keep her pregnant but I admit that's not got the best insurance policy and the second is to maintain my contacts within ACI and call in a favor if I have to. Hopefully, it won't come to that as I don't think it's something Cass really wants to do, anyway.

And to make it up to her I've got one of her Christmas presents already on order for a surprise. It won't bring Betsy back, but maybe her new-improved little sister (even smaller with more gadgets) will bring a smile to my girl's beautiful face.

Epilogue

★ ★ ★

Cassidy

2 years later

Damn baby-tuned super-hearing. I'm instantly awake when Bettina lets out a little test wail. I start to shift the blankets off so I can go convince her that people are supposed to sleep when it's dark, but Burke stops me with his impossibly long arm. "I'll get her. Go back to sleep, princess."

"Love you," I respond into my pillow, already heading back into that warm, timeless place. Until that is, the baby monitor picks up the one-sided conversation down the hall.

"Your mommy is a superhero. Did you know that, Betts? And I'm thinking you might be one too, the way you have me wrapped around your little fist. This one, right here. And then there's your tummy. It's too cute to resist." There several loud raspberries and Bettina's delighted giggles. Then Burke starts singing, off key and with mostly made up words. Something about lambs and oceans and…

I wake up to sunlight streaming in the long windows that take up an entire wall in the master bedroom. That hasn't happened in months. In fact, I'm not sure I've ever seen it this bright in here since we moved into the house right after my appendectomy. And I never would have guessed I'd be pregnant with our first child six months later, either. Although the way Burke has a habit of waking me up with a cup of coffee followed by slow and lazy morning sex might have had something to do with it. The man has taken laid-back charm to whole new depths. Literally.

My ears prick, listening for life in the house. There are faint sounds of activity coming from the general direction of the kitchen. Relieved, I stretch everything out in the big bed and then relax, staring up at the ceiling.

But I can only take that for so long, about ninety seconds, then I'm up on my feet and headed into the bathroom. God, I love this shower. It's like going to the spa. Dual shower heads with a tropical misting feature and a heated travertine bench. Burke has fucked me so sweetly on that bench so many times that I pretty much cum every time I look at it. It's heaven, absolute heaven even when I'm alone in here. Curiosity has me shutting down the taps and toweling off sooner than I might otherwise. What are those two getting up to?

A mess is what they're up to. Cream of wheat, at least I hope it's cream of wheat, is dripping off the table on to the tile floor and off of Betts's highchair and Burke's hair. But they both have matching grins on their faces, so I can't help but soak up the scene with a full heart. From a safe distance in the doorway. A little more white stuff goes flying when Bettina shakes her spoon in the air when she spots me. "Mama!" she shouts for the very first time ever.

Burke and I look at each other with wonder because clearly we've made the most clever child ever to grace the planet. And I think she really does have superpowers because here's the same high-octane athlete I accidentally found not that many months ago crouched down besides a highchair looking like he's the happiest he's ever been. That last doubt, the one that maybe he'd get bored with me eventually, with this, pops like a little soap bubble and just fades away. My smile gets a little misty because I'm just so damn happy.

"Cass? You alright over there? Sure you don't want to join us? Betts and I are seeing who can get the most breakfast on or in our target of choice."

"I'm good, thanks. But I can take over if you want to grab a shower now."

"Naw. Thought we'd do that together in about..." he glances down at his high-tech watch, "five minutes give or take."

"We can't leave the munchkin unattended."

"Not going to, are we, Betts?" he tweaks her little button nose, and she gazes up at him adoringly with round amber eyes. They are so freaking much alike, it's uncanny.

"Your mother is coming over to take her to see her new cousin for a few hours. There was some hard negotiating, but we settled on three hours as long as we put it towards another grandbaby."

I thunk my head into the doorjamb. "Please tell me you didn't really have that conversation with my mother?" I plead.

"It was implied. She did use the term 'another grandbaby'. I did say we could use some time alone and that it would be much appreciated if our own visit to see the new addition, for the second time, could be delayed for a few days. The clincher was uninterrupted grandma time with Princess Betts, here."

Just so we're clear we're not adding another baby to this delightful mix for at least another year. But if Burke wants to call it practice? For something where he's clearly not lacking skills, fine by me. I still can't believe my mother moved my dad and herself across the country just because my brother and I happened to land in the same town. Fine, I know it was the impending grandbabies that really did it. I like to think my mother wanted to see her youngest daughter, but we all know that's not worth more than a couple of visits a year. Bettina though? Yep, she can get people to up and move house.

I let Burke pull me against his side, smooshing into all the cream of wheat splatters and lose myself in his kiss while Bettina beats the tray of her high chair with her spoon in satisfaction. I sneak one hand up under his shirt just to see if he's gained a dad bod when I wasn't looking. Nope, just as hard and tight as ever. He smirks down at me like he knows just what I'm thinking. Or maybe it's because he thinks he's about to get lucky. Oh, fuck. It's both, and he knows it.

PREVIEW
BRAVING CASH

1

★ ★ ★

Sasha

Oh my God! I can't believe I'm sitting here with all these kick-ass women. Years ago when I was in college I did some temp work for a large company. But after graduation I took a job with a boutique marketing firm out in the hinterlands of the Peninsula before branching out on my own as a full-time freelancer. So I haven't been involved in the big corporate world or seen so many people in one room at the same time since then. It's somewhat intimidating, particularly when you consider that this is just a fraction of the people that are or will be here for their annual war games.

Looking around the large tent, I feel like a complete impostor. These women are confident. And I know they don't have a military background either but at least they're used to working with people that do. They know how to handle themselves and it shows. I'm a graphic designer. I know how to handle an art director having an overly dramatic hissy fit over video conference, but something tells me Alpha Corps runs to a completely different kind of drama. I take a deep breath in to steady myself.

I don't really belong here. I'm not even a regular ACI employee, I just got hired on in a temporary capacity because I'm Mia and Alexei's neighbor. And a neighbor to the property being used for the games so there's that. But basically I'm unskilled help when it comes to this event. And Mia had most everything to do with my being a part of it. She's not been very subtle about her intent to match make this summer, but I just smiled and shrugged my shoulders. The last ten years or so have proved I'm not irresistible to men and since I don't go in for one-night stands, I can almost guarantee nothing's going to happen. But Mia and Alexei are so damn cute together I don't want to spoil Mia's fun. She'll get tired of pushing men in front of me eventually, probably sooner if, as I expect, they all shrug and turn away. And if one didn't, well, maybe my pride would feel a little better, particularly if one Cash Travers were to be there to see it.

I sigh, inspecting the nails of my left hand. I need a manicure. A real one, not the chemical torture that passes for it at the Nailed It! Salon on Anemone Avenue. Even if one of the guys that are only here temporarily did ask me out, Cash probably wouldn't even notice. And if he did, wouldn't spare it a second thought. In the two weeks since I tried to ask him out myself and failed miserably, I still haven't been able to decide if it's more embarrassing to ask a guy out on a date and be turned down or for him to not comprehend that you were asking him out in the first place. I am absolutely not going back for a do-over to get a definitive answer on that one.

I glance across the giant tent to where Mia is resting her ever present clipboard on top of her just-showing baby bump. I'm kind of surprised it took them that long to have another kid. Every time Alexei asks me to watch the twins for an hour I get hot thinking about all the baby making activity going on in their house. The way he looks at his wife could start a forest fire in a driving rainstorm. Which isn't why I watch the twins, of course. The girls are adorable and I figure I should have some young pseudo nieces looking out for me when I'm old and gray (and still single).

No, the girls are just plain fun and we have a good time doing whatever they're into at the moment. Last time it was catching raindrops on our tongues. I can't wait to have a new baby to add to the mix. Because something tells me Alexei and Mia could have a houseful and *still* need the house to themselves for an hour or two (sometimes three) on a regular basis. They think I'm doing them a huge favor but really I'm getting my kid fix as part of coming to terms with the fact that it's increasingly unlikely I'll ever have a chance to have any of my own. I'm not prepared to go the single route on that one. Not yet.

Now I'm just getting maudlin, so I give myself a good shake and clap over-enthusiastically when the speaker finally stops talking and announces lunch.

"That bad, huh?" The woman next to me asks with a laugh.

I glance her way with a smile. "Honestly, I wasn't following much, but I needed to shake myself awake."

"You and me both. Hey, I'm Lennox, Lenny to my friends. Want to sit together at lunch?"

"Sasha and sure, that would be great." And just like that I'm back in middle school making friends in the lunchline on the first day of classes. Some things never change.

It turns out that because today is for the early arrivals, they don't even have the kitchen fully set up, so we get bagged lunches with simple sandwiches and pre-packaged food from a big box store. Lenny and I grab seats at the end of one of the big cafeteria tables.

"I'm not looking forward to eating this for the next two weeks." Lenny eyes her sandwich with puzzlement, peering at the pureed filling between the two triangles of bread.

I nod and take a tentative bite. I can't tell if it's chicken or tofu. The overwhelming taste of basil is disguising everything else. "I think I'll be eating at home. I need to go let my dog out, anyway."

Lenny's eyes widen. "You live here?"

I nod again, my curls bouncing. "Right next door. I'm really a graphic designer but they hired me to help out with the on the ground stuff. I think I'll be busy for the next few days and then not so busy and then frantic with wrap-up, getting everyone down to the boats for departure. That kind of thing."

"Well, I can see this would be a quiet place to raise a family. You got kids?" Lenny's expression is simply mild interest.

"No. I borrow Mia's sometimes. There aren't a lot of single men on the island. They can all make more money on the mainland so they don't have much reason to stay." I sigh wistfully, thinking of Cash. He'll head back to his unit soon, I'm sure, and then I'll probably not see him again. Not like I've seen too much of him recently. I'm too embarrassed to accidentally 'find him' around town again.

Lenny eyes me skeptically, like she can read my thoughts, but she just nods and keeps whatever she's thinking to herself. And I figure as long as nobody but me knows that Cash was oblivious to my overtures, then it never really happened, so I'm not keen to talk about it.

Cash

Embrace Island is a fucking weird place. Or maybe that should be weird fucking place. Because you can't. At least, not if you were raised on the island. Not without being talked about openly at the diner, or the post office, or the old men's gossip group down at the marina. And then there's the betting pool openly displayed in the hardware store behind the counter as to when the relationship will break up. Unless you follow *all* the rules. A buddy from high school once called it a cult. It's not but it can be a bit like the Amish without the old-fashioned clothes and out-dated farm equipment. I blame it on too many people seeing the same faces day after day during the winter months. They get bored. This is their idea of entertainment.

Tourists can do what they like and nobody blinks because they'll be gone before the snow falls. But locals… not so much. I thought that when I left the island at eighteen to join the Marines that I was done with all that shit. And no, I wasn't a virgin by the time I left, but then Gina Hennessy wasn't much for the rules either. Luckily for my parents' sake her name was already up on the board so she was never publicly linked with me. I still felt bad for her though and I hear she moved off island two years later when she got pregnant. I certainly don't feel an ounce of guilt when I occasionally hook up with a woman out in the real world. But then, in all of those previous cases, neither the woman nor I expected anything permanent or even very long term.

Coming back home on extended leave as a thirty-five-year-old man to visit my parents I wasn't expecting Sasha and I sure as hell wasn't expecting to get sucked back into the weird-ass customs of the place formerly known by a rather rude word relating to a woman's pussy. The name was changed when a group of shopkeepers formed a chamber of commerce and decided the brochure was likely to get banned on the mainland.

None of this is Sasha's fault. I'd bet a month's salary she doesn't even know this stuff goes on. She may have lived here for a few years, but you aren't a local unless the entire town has seen you in diapers. *And* your father in diapers too, and I don't mean the senior kind.

So I was more than a little aggravated when I was about to ask Sasha if she wanted to grab pie at the diner only to have my father pull me aside and inform me, "She lives here, son. You can't do that to her unless you take her to the hardware store first."

I remember blinking and clenching my jaw in rage. Until common sense sunk in and I realized Dad was right. I don't live here anymore, but if I take Sasha out without following local customs, I'll be making life difficult for her after I leave. Because they all know that I know the rules, so the locals will assume

I'm treating her like a hooker, even if we don't fuck or even kiss. And I am leaving. I've got three more weeks left of leave having had to wait a few years to be free to take any, but then I'm reporting to duty in Hawaii.

A smart man would simply sidestep the curvy woman with the sexy blonde curls and move on with his life. But I can't seem to get her out of my head.

At the same time officially declaring my intent to 'court' Sasha seems dishonest. I just want to take the woman out. Okay, I wouldn't turn down fucking her if she was open to it, because she's seriously hot in that completely unaware of it way. It's obvious that flirting and dressing to attract a man aren't high on her priority list because she has a million other things she's into and thinking about. For some reason that makes me want to follow her around, to be the one that catches her attention and wins her smiles. But I'm not looking for a wife. Not anytime soon, and probably not ever. Definitely not with the entire island watching my every move.

So I'm leaving her alone. Even if my eyes track for a hint of her presence everywhere I go. I haven't seen her for a few weeks, which makes me wonder if she's okay. I'm about ready to ask my sister if she's heard anything when I hear Sasha's name being mentioned in the booth kitty-corner to mine. I slide over just an inch so I can see who's talking. This is my dad's pub so I've been hanging out in the back corner, nursing a pint and catching up with the family in between customers. I offered to help, but my mom pushed me down into the booth and frowned at me until I gave in.

The couple next door is curiously out of place on this island. Or at least they would have been fifteen years ago. Things are clearly changing. The man looks vaguely familiar, and the woman is pretty and glowingly pregnant. I know this mostly because the man keeps telling her, "Mia, eat. The baby needs it." Her reply is so automatic I don't think she even thinks before she speaks, "Alexei, I'm fine. The baby is fine. Stop fussing. I love you."

Alexei. That's when it comes to me, why he looks familiar. I've heard of him. He's legendary in the dark world of military cyber warfare. They say he could find out what you're thinking long before your brain forms the sentences. He retired a few years ago but people still talk about him. It's hard to reconcile that shadowy persona with the man currently forcing french fries on his wife.

His wife, on the other hand, is not as impressed with his accomplishments as I am. Odds are good, she doesn't even know most of it. "So, did you see anyone that would be a good fit for Sasha? I was kind of thinking about Oldham but then I found out he doesn't believe in wearing deodorant." She wrinkles her nose in disgust.

Alexei sighs, "Leaver her alone, Mia. If she even

wants to find a man Sasha is perfectly capable of doing so on her own."

"Piff." Mia dismisses that with a wave of her hand. "Where, exactly? There's like five single men over eighteen on this island normally and none of them will do. You're just worried about losing your babysitter."

I watch, fascinated, as he leans closer to his wife and whispers something that has her smiling and blushing a fiery red all at the same time.

She gets back on her agenda pretty fast though. "Well, if you aren't going to help, I'm going to spend some time tomorrow at breakfast looking the crowd over. You can get the girls ready for the day. There's got to be the perfect man for her in there somewhere."

That's when something in my gut twists in anger. How dare this woman try to steal my girl away for some other guy? Sasha is mine. I'm halfway out of my seat to set her straight when reality hits and I sink back down, stunned.

— Find out what happens next in Braving Cash Book 3 of ACI Unleashed

Thank you for reading!

Get another peek into the world of ACI with Lucy who has her own adventure with a modern day Viking/Swedish Special Forces soldier. Get her story when you sign up for my newsletter.

https://BookHip.com/ZNBSVAS

About Me

I write lighthearted steamy romance featuring alphalicious heroes who know what they want and strong, smart heroines that can spot gold underneath a tough exterior.

My promise to you: no cheating, always an HEA, and more than a few silly bits.

I love my characters and I want them all to live happily ever after (along with fabulous careers, chubby babies, and/or adorable pets.) Sometimes this requires letting go of how the real world works. I'm okay with that and I hope you are too!

I live and work in the wilds of the Pacific Northwest where I like to experiment with making wine and sourdough bread when I'm not writing or being lectured by my adorably entitled chickens.

Looking For More?

Grab this printable reading list that has what's out, what's coming, and what formats are available.

https://tinyurl.com/OliviaBooks

That presumes I've updated it! And if you think I might have forgotten or even to just say hi, you can reach me at: oliviasinclairbooks@gmail.com. I love hearing from readers and I do my best to respond to everyone.

www.ingramcontent.com/pod-product-compliance
Lightning Source LLC
Chambersburg PA
CBHW020821190726
48285CB00006B/2371